Blood Pudding

Blood Pudding

Art Corriveau

ESPLANADE
Books

THE FICTION SERIES AT VÉHICULE PRESS

Esplanade Books editor: Andrew Steinmetz

Cover design: David Drummond
Set in Adobe Minion and Berling by Simon Garamond
Photograph of the author by Timothy Horn
Printed by Marquis Printing Inc.

LIBRARY AND ARCHIVES CANADA CATALOGUING IN PUBLICATION

Corriveau, Art
Blood pudding / Art Corriveau.

Short stories.
ISBN 978-1-55065-228-4

I. Title.

PS3603.0685B56 2007   813'.6   C2007-904436-0

Published by Véhicule Press, Montréal, Québec, Canada
www.vehiculepress.com

Distribution in Canada: LitDistCo
orders@lpg.ca

Distribution US: Independent Publishers Group
www.ipgbook.com

Printed in Canada on 100% post-consumer recycled paper.

Contents

Blood Pudding

PAUL SMELLS CLOVES and sees Mémère. She slices through years of forgetting: the flash of piano wire through a pig's throat. A whiff of cloves and the cast-iron pot is again aboil behind the toolshed. And Mémère is stooped over it, pouring sap buckets of blood into the thickening. He can see her, shrouded in woodsmoke, a finger dipping into the pot then disappearing, crimson into her mouth. She adds a handful of cloves or fennel, sage. The stench of cloves will linger for weeks, a caul on all their faces. It will remain long after she has returned to Quebec, long after the high-pitched squeals have faded from his dreams.

Paul is sitting at Isabelle's kitchen table, uncomfortable in such heavy clothes. His body hasn't felt this cold in years. He watches his twin sister, dusted in flour, rolling out cookie dough. She is humming something he doesn't know. On the stove: oranges, lemons, dates and raisins simmered in apple juice, cooling now in a stainless soup pot. Isabelle is making vegetarian mincemeat cookies for their Thanksgiving dinner. She has assured Paul they will not be having turkey. Cloves and cinnamon have condensed into droplets on the panes. He tries not to think about flinging all the windows open. His sister's apartment is cold enough.

He is surprised by how much grayer her hair is. His own is still quite red—what's left of it. He searches this ghost of a child's face for signs of Isabelle, a sassy little girl with freckles. They once looked like opposite-sexed versions of each other. Now they look like strangers. They are strangers. Relieved, he notices she still bites the tip of her tongue when she concentrates. Their mother used to joke: the minute Isabelle's brain goes on, her tongue comes out. Isabelle's *pisette*, their father liked to call it.

"When do the folks get in from Florida?" he asks.

"Tomorrow morning," she says, cutting circles of dough by pressing an empty coffee can into it. "We pick them up at Dorval around half past ten. United."

They speak in English, the language of their childhood. French would now be easier for both of them. Isabelle has lived in Montreal for twenty years; he, in Burkina Faso for almost twenty-five. He wonders what will be spoken when his parents arrive. They have recently sold the farm in Vermont and retired to Fort Lauderdale where they probably speak more French than English—*Montréal du Sud*. His father still thinks of himself as Québécois, though he has now lived more of his life in the States. His mother is indifferent, American.

He hopes they will all speak English. That's where most of his happiness is recorded, in English.

When his whole world was the farm in Vermont, before he and Isabelle were made to go to school, he thought every family was like theirs. He thought everyone was blessed with a set of grandparents: jolly, English-speaking elderly who brought gifts with them from Massachusetts. He also thought everyone was cursed with a mémère: an ancient Québécoise who materialized, as if by sorcery, at the first scent of slaughter. It was Paul's second-grade teacher who finally explained that "grandmother" and "mémère" meant the same thing. The possibilities of translation would never have occurred to him on his own—in French he thought one way, in English another.

"What have we got planned for today?" Paul asks Isabelle. There are still so many aunts and uncles, cousins to visit before his return to Africa. Isabelle is now spooning the warm mincemeat onto cookie circles, folding the dough over to make plump half-moons. It is Paul's job to tamp down the edges with the tines of a fork. But that smell! He doubts he will be able to choke down a single cookie by the time they're baked.

"How about the gallery?" she says. "I need to stop by to sign a few forms. It would give you a chance to see my recent work."

"Sounds good," Paul says. This is a lie. He doesn't like his sister's art. Has no desire to read her mind. "What about tonight?"

"How about holing up here, getting good and drunk? Unless priests don't do that."

Paul laughs. "What other options does a priest have on a Tuesday night?"

A cobra rears up from the red dust of the trail. Paul and Jean-Baptiste are deep in discussion, strategizing how they will get the Catholic Church to pay for smallpox vaccinations in Jean-Baptiste's village, just around the bend. Jean-Baptiste advocates using the funds reserved for an annual shipment of *Safeguards to Chastity*; the villagers are in the habit of offering the manual's thin, soft pages as guest toilet paper. Paul understands this but is uncomfortable falsifying even one line of the parish budget. Jean-Baptiste counters with an axiom in Dyula, the dialect of commerce: the best tools for telling the truth are not often the facts. They do not notice the cobra until it is too late, until it hisses and fans its magnificent hood. They are mesmerized, silent. Silence along the Volta.

Then, before Jean-Baptiste can warn Paul to turn away, the cobra takes aim. It spits. Paul is blinded. Acid in his eyes, searing pain that brings him to his knees. Above his own frantic cries, Paul can hear Jean-Baptiste crying out in dialect for help, can hear Jean-Baptiste's machete hacking, hacking at the snake.

Villagers arrive. They chatter too excitedly for Paul to follow what is happening. He feels himself lifted to his feet by many hands, then lifted entirely off the ground, over many heads.

He is a coffin.

The drum of bare feet on the dust, more excited cries, the familiar smells of dog and cooking fire and dried thatching. The sun disappears. Noise is muffled. Coolness and the smell of cool earth. He is set down on a bed of corn husks covered with blankets, the smell of dog even stronger than before.

Jean-Baptiste whispers in his ear, in French: lie still; there is only one cure for this; keep very still; help is on the way; shall we pray together?

It has not occurred to Paul to pray. Sightless, a coffin, he has not thought of God. Paul wonders at this lack of interest in the destiny of his own soul. Has he reached a state of selflessness or one of apathy? Jean-Baptiste begins: *Notre Père, qui est au ciel, que votre nom soit sanctifié, que votre règne vienne…* The Africans still *vouvoyer* God, insist on it. Common courtesy extended to a visitor.

Several villagers enter the hut. Jean-Baptiste leaves off praying and instructs Paul to lie very still. Paul's hands are pried away from his face. Gentle fingers hold his lids open while someone, a woman, straddles his chest. Freshly shucked corn husks, cola berries, vaginal mysteries. Then, finally, there is relief: a warm liquid dribbled into his eyes to wash the acid away. It trickles down the ridge of Paul's nose, across his lips.

After several repetitions of this bath, his sight begins to return. He tries to focus on a silent decade of Hail Marys, a tribute to her mercy. But his mind keeps wandering to the cobra's eyes. His grandmother's eyes. Slowly, he begins to recognize Jean-Baptiste's niece astride his chest. She is smiling down at him. Marie-Thérèse. He has just baptized her baby boy, not more than a week ago. He cannot recall the baby's Christian name, though it must surely be one of the apostles'.

"*Ça va mieux?*" Marie-Thérèse asks, still clutching her right breast, stained now with pearly drops of milk meant for her son.

Isabelle's show is at a warehouse gallery in Old Monreal. They have decided to walk there from her apartment in Chinatown. Even worse than the wind, Paul decides, is the lack of light. He has forgotten how Quebec is unable to manage more than an overcast twilight in November. He doubts he could ever get used to this again, the gloom. But shrinking into the parka borrowed from his sister, he reminds himself he had better.

The gallery seems suffocatingly warm compared to outside. Someone, a man named André, offers to take Paul's coat. Paul shakes his hand. He can't see this André because his glasses have fogged over. (He rarely wears these in Africa except when he's reading or saying mass. His life there doesn't require much attention to detail.) André claims to own the gallery, has heard so much about him, disappears with the coats. Isabelle bursts into a fit of giggles. She tells Paul not to move; she'll be right back with a tissue.

Isabelle doesn't come right back, nor does André. Paul is left to wipe his glasses on his shirttail and explore the gallery on his own. He wonders if they are lovers, Isabelle and André. He doesn't know why, but he suspects they are. Twins. In the foyer are several benign paintings by contemporary artists. The work seems pleasant, derivative: urban landscapes in muddy watercolours, abstract dribbles in layered acrylics, oversize mixed media collages. Paul is certainly no art expert. But he does visit all the museums whenever he is on leave in Paris or Rome or New York. What else can a priest do on vacation? Obvious answer: he can visit his family. None of this work is Isabelle's. Her installation is featured behind a white partition.

These days, Isabelle upholsters furniture with gore—with the skin and hair and guts of slaughtered animals. For this installation, she has arranged a living room. The sofa is covered in badly sewn-together pig carcasses with a Victorian pattern shaved into the bristles. Entrails poke out of the seams, enormous cow tongues serve as bolsters. Next to the sofa, an easy chair of carelessly plucked chicken skins. Delicate doilies adorn the armrests, crocheted and beaded out of pigs' teeth. The coffee table is made from sheep limbs, the hooves still on them. The bladder lampshade is fringed with hanks of a horse's mane. The floor is splattered in blood, buckets of it. On the wall, framed by dozens of eyeballs, is a photograph of Mémère.

Paul whirls around, afraid he might be sick. He nearly collides into his sister who stands behind him, watching.

"What do you think?" she asks.

"Air," gasps Paul. "I need air."

Back in the foyer, André explains how Isabelle's medium is latex, the material from which movie masks are made. Paul has seen few movies in his adult life; his parish is in the bush, kilometers from Ouagadougou. While André chatters on about clay forms and molded rubber, Isabelle smokes a cigarette across the room and stares out the window. Paul sips a glass of water and pretends to be listening to

André. But he can't seem to keep himself anchored to the stone bench. It is not the here and now. It is the eve of slaughter.

And the twins are playing Mille Bornes in the tree-house their father has built for them. And until this moment, it has been summer. But suddenly a cold gust sends a shiver through the giant maple: the first creaks of winter. And they know. They know without peeking into the barnyard that she has appeared with the wind. But they peek anyway. And there she is, rising up out of the settling dust—hands on her hips, directing one of the Canadian uncles to set her bags on the porch. They hide in the tree-house until their father calls them down.

Mémère doesn't hug them, she never kisses them. She addresses them only in French, and never individually. She keeps her distance. Her you's are plural, formal. Because she cannot drive a car, there is always some poor uncle along to do her bidding. The twins hold each other's hand to be able to stare up at her. A mountain of flesh, skin stretched over two hundred pounds, features beginning to sag and sweat like carved altar candles in August. Iron-gray hair, a helmet of Orphan Annie curls. Wire-framed glasses with thick flashing lenses, glasses magnifying jet black eyes beyond all human proportions, the eyes of a horsefly. They are mesmerized until she prompts them to speak: "*Vous vous en souvenez de votre oncle Raymond.*" You remember your uncle Raymond. They nod politely, respond: "*Bonjour mon oncle,*" though one Canadian uncle looks much the same as another.

Isabelle interrupts André. "We should be going. We have to make the rounds with the relatives." André asks Paul to excuse the two of them, he and Isabelle have a little business to conclude, they won't be a moment. Paul nods.

Outside, the clouds break for a few moments of fitful sunlight that brightens the cobbled sidewalks and granite buildings. Paul fingers the black canker on the back of his neck. His hair is red, his skin freckled. Not a complexion well suited to equatorial sun.

Their uncle Raymond does not leave his apartment now. Emphysema. He is unable to climb the winding wrought-iron staircase. Paul has forgotten this odd quirk of Montreal: winding front staircases, little more than narrow fire escapes that belong in back. As they wait for

Raymond to answer the door, Paul wonders why his uncle has not moved to the first floor of some other building.

The hunched little man who greets them bears no resemblance to anyone Paul remembers. He wonders if his father will also look this old. He hasn't seen his parents in nearly five years. He has no mental image of them as elderly. "*C'est moi, Paul*," he says, hoping to jog his uncle's memory. Paul, a name that can be pronounced one way in Montreal, another in Vermont.

Raymond squints at him and, in a husky voice, says he has not called for a priest; he feels fine today. Paul has forgotten he is wearing his collar. He doesn't bother with one in Africa. Just a white tunic. In the bush, his skin colour gives him away immediately as a priest. Businessmen from France always seem to wear khaki. Isabelle steps forward and hugs Raymond, explaining who Paul is. He pats her on the back and lets Paul enter, though he is clearly suspicious about the arrival of the Church. Isabelle whispers to Paul that Raymond is often like this—has his good days and his bad days.

The apartment smells lonely: leftover food on the brink of spoiling, reworn clothes that are tidy but not clean. The place smells to Paul like a man resigned to spending the rest of his life without companionship. The twins sit on the sofa; Raymond sits formally, his back erect in a well-worn armchair. Paul inquires about Raymond's health, learns that it is as good as can be expected. No one speaks again until Isabelle jumps up, offering to make them all tea. Another quirk of Paul's family: tea drinkers, not coffee drinkers. Paul tries to quell an uncalled-for flush of panic. He drinks coffee in Burkina Faso, strong black coffee. Why does he feel so afraid Raymond's aloneness will suffocate him? He listens anxiously for Isabelle, hears her putting the kettle on in the kitchen. She knows her way around. "You are the one who lives in Africa," Raymond says, suddenly remembering, though Isabelle has just explained this to him at the door. He uses the formal you with Paul, the familiar one with Isabelle.

"Yes, I live in Africa," Paul says, relieved.

"You didn't take over the farm in Vermont. You entered the priesthood."

"Yes. I answered the calling."

"And it still suits you?"

Paul is not sure whether Raymond is referring to Africa or the priesthood. The obvious answer is yes, it still suits him. But for some reason, staring at this uncle who will soon die, he decides to tell him: test out the words, the secret he must eventually reveal to Isabelle and his parents.

"I'm leaving Africa, uncle. It's my skin. The doctors say it can't take the sun much longer. I will soon be transferred back to America, to Montreal perhaps."

Raymond nods.

"Here we are," says Isabelle. She has returned with a tray. She sets it on the coffee table: three mugs of steaming water, a saucer of Red Rose teabags, a sugar bowl, a ceramic creamer in the shape of a cow. "I forgot *ma tante* had this," she says to Raymond, lifting the creamer. "For special occasions." Isabelle holds the cow almost lovingly, pours milk from its mouth. She begins to recount the stringent social habits of her aunt, dead now for nearly a dozen years.

The creamer looks more like a pig than a cow.

And as Isabelle coaxes milk from it, Paul finds himself sitting on the top rail of the sty fence. It is autumn. The twins sit side by side, watching while their father and Raymond garrote all but two of the pigs. They watch dry-eyed and silent, the sharp air saturated with dead leaves and shrill squeals. Mémère stands by, of course, with the sap buckets. She catches the gushing blood by clamping them over the heads of the dying, struggling pigs. She is dressed in a house frock and apron; rubber barn boots and pastel rubber gloves. She will take the buckets, still steaming, over to her bubbling kettle out behind the toolshed.

"And your husband?" Raymond asks during a lull in Isabelle's chatter. "He is well?" Silence.

"I suppose," Isabelle says. "But you've forgotten, *mon oncle*. I'm divorced, for years now."

Raymond nods. "Your father, then. He is well?"

"Flying up from Florida tomorrow. To see Paul. It's American Thanksgiving."

Another nod. "Ah. Your mother. You celebrate those holidays."

Paul watches his mother float across the barnyard, a pitcher of iced tea in one hand, several glasses clamped together in the fingers of the other. Quiet, slender, the most beautiful woman in the world. She offers tea to Raymond who drinks it all, handing the empty glass back without a word. She smiles anyway and moves on to refresh her husband. Paul can sometimes see her in the vegetable garden or rocking on the orchard swing. But he cannot picture her inside the house. He cannot picture anything about the house's insides—how the kitchen is, the furniture.

They have been raised to be outdoor children. Their mother calls them her little barn cats; she insists they play outside as soon as the snow melts. This they do by making the spring piglets their toys, by dividing the brood into Paul's and Isabelle's. Isabelle dresses her half in dolls' clothes, chauffeuring them around in an old baby buggy. She talks to them in their language, insists she understands. She tries to teach them English while she bottle-feeds them or arranges elaborate tea parties in their honour. She will admit that English gives them trouble—their snouts aren't properly formed to make the sounds. But they try hard. She never names them. She knows better.

Paul can't understand why Isabelle chooses to fall in love with her piglets each spring. He bosses his own half of the brood around, cracking a willow whip across their backs, making them run races across the pen. Isabelle insists that it is okay to love them—as long as they don't have names. There will always be more, she insists.

Back on the fence, Paul wonders where his mother is. He can only see Mémère. Is she in the orchard as each nameless pig is garroted? In the house?

His mug of tea. He notices the milk from that ceramic cow has curdled into tiny maggots floating on top. Raymond finishes his tea unaware, sets his empty mug onto the floor. "Well. Then. Welcome home, Father," he says. Time for them to go. Raymond does not ask Paul for a blessing. Paul does not offer one.

Paul dribbles water on baby Thomas's forehead. *Je te baptise, Thomas, dans le nom du Père, du Fils et du Saint-Esprit*. The baby begins to scream as Paul attempts to explain to him—and all those gathered—how he must live the rest of his life as a good Catholic. Eventually, he hands Thomas over to his mother, Marie-Thérèse. She quiets him by offering her breast. Paul has been dreading this baptism for a week. Marie-Thérèse's uncle, Jean-Baptiste, is an elder of the village. They will surely serve meat at the feast.

Besides the infrequent dog that dies, meat is only eaten on special occasions—baptisms and burials—events at which Paul is always present as a guest of honour. He loves his parishioners too much to offend them by refusing the choicest slabs of python or elephant trunk or rhinoceros horn. He has suffered numerous bouts of tapeworm and dysentery over the years. Monkey and buffalo and crocodile.

Mercifully, droughts and civilization have driven the game animals deep into the Congo. When Paul first arrived in Burkina Faso (then the newly independent nation of Upper Volta), he believed his mission was to save souls. But as the governments came and went—the Yamégos, the Lamizanas; the Zerbos, Campaorés and Sankaras—he began to recognize the futility of this until he saved a few lives. The conversion of savannas to cotton, sugar and peanut plantations displacing the lion prides and jackals. Looking back, he realizes he has converted many more hunters to farmers than heathens to Catholics. Corn, at least, was something the bush could use. All those years in seminary to become a farmer, like his father.

The baptism mass is over before his mind has fully caught up with the words. Baptisms and burials. The only time prayers seem to tumble out effortlessly.

He walks with his congregation to the feast. The sun is slowly cooking his skin. He is the antelope now turning, turning on a spit in Jean-Baptiste's family compound. Paul is seated at the head of a Western-style table that is set up outside, near the spit. Small talk is tricky at such inter-village events. He finds himself commenting on crops and inoculation programs in the Mande languages of Samo and Marka, drifting now and then into the Moré dialects of the Lobi, Bibo, and Garunsi. At the table is where he begins to pray in earnest—when the words are not just meaningless poetry, but heartfelt pleas.

He begs God in English, to please, please allow him to eat graciously. But his prayers are silenced when a leg joint is set in front of him. He cannot hear the laughter and chatter around him. He cannot hear his own pleas to heaven. Because his fate rests on a plate before him. Because he must tear the flesh away from the bone. He must chew and swallow it with every eye and every smile of the village upon him. He must not gag, must not gag when the juices, the cooked blood, explode in his mouth.

"How is Jean-Marc?" Paul asks Isabelle. They are waiting for a train in the Berri metro station. The cold. Paul can't seem to keep from shuddering.

"I don't know," says Isabelle. "Married again. Living in Burlington. He owns a Texaco station." She is examining a poster of a painfully thin woman luxuriating on a sofa in a full-length mink; the mink has casually fallen open to prove she needs only a lacy bra and panties beneath it. The slogan in bold type over her head: *Bien Dans Sa Peau.* Comfortable in her skin. Paul notices it and occupies himself by trying to make the slogan work in English. He can't. But translation is a hard habit to break. It has been an obsession since childhood— this trying to glue together two halves of a life through language.

Paul thinks of his father. Comfortable in his skin. Paul is ten and insists on following him around the barn after school. He dresses in the same overalls, wears smaller versions of the green rubber boots. But he cannot be his father, a gentle man and a murderer all wrapped up in the same person. He cannot see how those halves fit together. It is winter, snowing. Paul is helping his father feed the cows when he stumbles upon a translation that leads him to the priesthood. *Manger* means to eat. Farm animals eat out of a manger, the crib of baby Jesus.

Above the din of the approaching train, Isabelle shouts into Paul's ear that she has invited André to dinner, she hopes he doesn't mind. Paul nods as they board the nearest carriage. He wonders when they will talk. For now, he is comforted by the rocking motion of the train. Isabelle's first husband Jean-Marc. A very nice, very simple man who moved out to the farm after the wedding; moved into Isabelle's bedroom, began helping out with the chores. The folks were by then tired of farming: waking up at five every morning to milk the Holsteins and slop the pigs. Farming was exactly what Jean-Marc wanted to do.

Paul received snapshots in the mail their first year of marriage. Jean-Marc with his arm around Isabelle, standing in front of the tree-house maple; Jean-Marc's eyes on her, her eyes on the camera. Jean-Marc and their father grinning and dressed in hunter plaid, flanking the trunk of the old Chevy; two dead deer strapped to the trunk, their eyes staring into the camera. Jean-Marc and their father shirtless, muscular, grinning again; this time in front of the pigsty, piano wires glistening in autumn sun. More photos of the two men than of the newlyweds.

Just before their second anniversary, Isabelle ran away from home. She turned up in Canada—at Mémère's—a couple of weeks later. Got a job in an art supply store. Took night courses. Jean-Marc stayed on for a while, until the folks told him he would have to leave the farm.

When Paul and Isabelle exit the metro, they see a crowd gathered around a street performer. It's a magician dressed in a ridiculous black cape. He appears to be mixing a cake in his stovepipe hat; cracking eggs, pouring milk. Isabelle suggests they watch for a minute. Paul agrees—this sort of thing has always entranced her—though he would much rather buy a fifth of whiskey and soak in a scalding tub until dinner. He wraps the borrowed scarf a little more tightly around his neck.

A tap of the magician's wand on the hat brim produces a white rabbit instead of a cake. Isabelle claps her hands and laughs, once again his ten-year-old sister. Little Isabelle, enthusiastic about any sort of escape. Paul searches the sky for a break in the clouds. They are seamless. For the magician's next trick he needs a volunteer, a lovely assistant. Isabelle waves her hand. A large, floppy hat covers most of her hair, a toothy grin and sparkling eyes transform her into a lovely assistant. The magician points to her and she steps forward, willingly. He tells her to bring along her handsome friend. She grabs Paul's arm and drags him into the center of attention.

The magician gives Isabelle the rabbit to hold while he instructs

Paul to help him set a black lacquer box on the table. He asks them where they are from. Isabelle says Paris, though her accent is clearly Québécois. She tells him they are both dancers in the Folies Bergère, dance partners on vacation. Are they married? No, Paul is her rich old uncle. The crowd whistles and howls. Paul wonders at Isabelle's facility for lies. He wishes he weren't wearing a scarf so everyone could see his collar. It makes him ashamed, this desire to hide behind the priesthood. The magician insists on seeing part of their dance act before he continues his trick. After all, he says, it isn't every day the Folies Bergère gets to Montreal. He encourages the crowd to clap and chant for a cancan. Isabelle hands the rabbit back to him. She turns to Paul and holds out her hand. "Join me," she whispers in English. It roars in his ears, this tiny invitation, drowns out the clamour of a sizable crowd that has gathered. He could still take off his scarf. He could still take it off and put an end to this. But instead he steps forward. The crowd cheers.

The magician, making conductor motions with the rabbit's paws, begins humming "Can You Do the Cancan?" The crowd picks up the melody and claps along in time. Paul throws his arm around Isabelle's shoulder and they begin to kick. The faster the crowd claps, the faster they kick, kicking wildly, first right and then left, faster and faster. Finally they stumble, and it is over. The magician makes them take a bow, crying, "Direct from the Folies Bergère, ladies and gentlemen, *messieurs-dames!*" The crowd roars its approval. Isabelle reaches up and cups Paul's face in her hands. "Thank you," she says. She smiles and kisses him lightly on the lips.

The trick continues. The magician hands the rabbit back to Isabelle. Then he makes Paul inspect the box, inside and out. The crowd laughs every time Paul carries out an instruction—Isabelle herself is nearly doubled over with mirth. Paul knows he is being ridiculed behind his back. He can see out of the corners of his eyes the magician's grotesque pantomimes. But he hams it up anyway, plays the fool—the rich old uncle.

After Isabelle places the rabbit in the box, she is told to pet it through a small opening in the top. Then the magician makes Paul don the black cape and hat (no sign of eggs or milk) to wave a wand over the box. He is flushed from the dancing, feels warm for the first time since his arrival. At the magician's prompting, Paul repeats a litany of off-colour incantations. He even decides to extemporize a little, adding a bit of Latin from Sunday mass—a benediction most of the crowd recognizes and applauds. Grinning and crossing himself, the magician opens the box. A dove flutters out. Isabelle swears she is still petting the rabbit, though the box looks empty. Paul tingles from the mystery of it all. The dove flies up, disappearing over the rooftops into the seamless gray sky.

Paul watches Isabelle at work. They are sipping a dry chardonnay at her studio space about a block away from her apartment. He has seated himself in a threadbare armchair over by the windows—to keep out of her way, he has told her. They both remember his squeamishness at the gallery. Isabelle is standing at a long plywood table set up on sawhorses in the middle of the room. She is trying to transform the forearm of a mannequin into a candelabra. Her idea is to melt slender wax tapers onto each of the fingertips. But it's not working; the candles keep toppling off before she can get them to drip properly. The sky has cleared somewhat for sunset. Paul is enjoying the heat streaming through the windows. Without really thinking about it, he suggests they carve little hollows into the bottom of each taper with his penknife. Isabelle hands him five fresh candles, joking it's about time he earned his keep. She switches to gluing hair bristles onto an elaborate centerpiece of mannequin limbs and lacquered rotting fruit. Her latest project: a formal banquet.

Paul finds himself humming the cancan song as he scrapes out the candles. He listens as Isabelle chatters about the Thanksgiving meal she will prepare for the folks. Paul is astonished by the complexity of each dish; it is not the food of their childhood: cheddar cheese and walnut soup, an eggplant gratin in a saffron custard, green beans marinated in a raspberry vinaigrette, salad greens with apples and oranges and raisins. Where do these cooking skills come from? He has never learned how to cook himself; has always been fed, in one way or another, by the Catholic Church—either by refusing the main meat course in the dining halls of seminary or by requesting spicy yogurts and vegetable stews from Marie-Magdeleine, his cook. At home in Africa, his sole responsibility at mealtime is to say grace for the three of them: Marie-Magdeleine, Sangoulé the housekeeper, and himself. He always adds a silent thank you for cultures of forced vegetarianism.

Somehow Isabelle has found a way to enjoy food—preparing it, eating it. It has something to do with these latex grotesqueries, he realizes, with the horrific confections of this studio. And suddenly he can see his mother's kitchen, for the first time in years: bouquets of dried spices and cast-iron pots hanging from the ceiling, an enormous white enamel cooking stove, dull maple floors and braided rugs, a plank table. The rocking chair. And there is Mémère, sitting at the table, scraping every possible shard of meat off the half-skull of a pig—the sharp teeth of its jawbone leering up at her. She is making head-cheese for the holidays; supervising her grandchildren. And there they are, the two of them, their hands stained a deep vermilion. Isabelle holds the gut casings steady while Paul grabs handfuls of the moist brown loam from Mémère's cast-iron pot and stuffs the casings to bursting. The smell of cloves and curdled blood. Blood pudding. *Boudin*. He is crying. Mémère tells him to stop acting like a girl.

"What's wrong?" Isabelle asks. Her fingertips are covered in brown bristles and she is staring at him. Paul realizes he has stopped carving candles, is staring at her.

"Your artwork," he says. "It's so violent."

"Growing up on a farm, I guess," she sighs. "Better to have it splashed all over the walls of a gallery than splashed all over the insides of my head."

"Is that why you do it?"

"Sure. When it bothers me."

"It was pretty horrible," Paul says.

"It was just a farm, Paul," Isabelle says. "Farms are like that. I can make pretty things, too."

Paul considers this. "I have cancer," he says. He is surprised by his abruptness, his matter-of-factness. He gets up from the armchair, wax shavings clinging to his trouser legs. He wants to come closer, reduce the distance between them. "Melanoma. The sun. They're sending me back to the States for treatment. Maybe here to Montreal. I'm meeting with the archbishop on Friday to discuss my options. I'm having more tests on Saturday, over at Hôtel-Dieu."

Isabelle sits down, sighs. "I figured. Sudden family visit, the spots." She touches the back of her own neck, leaving a few hairs sticking there. "How serious is it?"

Paul shrugs. "They think it's the kind they can cure. But I can't stay in the Volta. I'll be turning my parish over to a colleague, an African, at the end of the year."

"Do the folks know?"

Paul shakes his head.

"They're going to want you to request a transfer to Florida," Isabelle says. Paul smiles. She taps her forehead with the heel of her hand. "Oh, right; the sun, Isabelle. Out of the frying pan and into the fire." There isn't a trace of humour in her voice.

The door buzzer sounds. Both are startled. Then Isabelle gets up to take her brother into her arms. They fit together, two pieces of a whole. A good minute goes by before the buzzer sounds again. Wiping her hands on her apron, Isabelle crosses the room to let André in. Paul remains motionless among the arms and legs of Isabelle's banquet.

Because Jean-Baptiste has no children, the wedding feast of his niece, Marie-Thérèse, is one of the biggest the village has ever seen. Paul donates two cases of very good Médoc to the festivities. Such donations are sanctioned as community relations measures, at the discretion of the priest. The two cases are part of a quarterly shipment from France, the wine he generally blesses during mass. The blood of Christ.

After the Catholic ceremony, Paul makes sure he keeps moving from table to table, proposing toasts. In this way, no one notices that he has barely touched his meal. He is getting quite drunk. By the time the dancing begins, Paul realizes he must sit down or topple over. Very dignified, he thinks.

He loves the dancing: storytelling with movement and gesture;

drum rhythms dictating which secrets the body, not the mind, will tell. Marie-Thérèse is at the center of the dance, thrashing and swaying, laughing and groaning. To the delight of the revelers, her husband joins her. He begs her to marry him. She refuses, demanding to know what he could possibly offer her, Queen of the Bush. He plies her with promises of gifts: the earth, the rain, the sun, his seed. Finally she relents, accepts his proposal. A shout rises up from the dancers. The two are truly married.

Paul is given Jean-Baptiste's bed. It is customary, a politeness. Paul accepts the offer because he has had too much wine to wander back to the rectory on his own. He accepts the bed because he knows his friend, his dearest friend in Africa, will not be put out. Jean-Baptiste will drink and feast and dance with the others for two days, maybe more, without bothering with sleep.

Paul wakes to the sound of love-making. Marie-Thérèse and her new husband are consummating their marriage in the adjacent hut. He tries not to picture what they are doing, tries to complete a decade of the rosary. But his mind is too full of wine, too full of images from the dance. At seminary in Vermont, many of the novices would drive into Burlington on the weekends, to drink in bars where they might meet girls or boys for a night of company. Paul was never very well liked because he stayed in his room or went home to the farm. Some of his crueler classmates called him Father-Holier-Than-Thou. This was easier to bear than the truth: that women, their sex, terrified him.

As Marie-Thérèse approaches climax, so does Paul. His breath comes to him in the same short gasps. He finds himself adopting the rhythm of her husband. Their cries! He pictures her husband's seed shooting up inside her, into her very being, a holy thing. But he feels shame when his own seed spills, wasted, onto the cool earth of the hut's floor.

They have just finished dinner and André asks what's for dessert. Isabelle tells him nothing, the mince cookies are for company. André winks at Paul and begins to open another bottle of wine. They are back at Isabelle's apartment. Paul has eaten two helpings of spinach ravioli followed by a big plate of salad. His appetite pleases him. He likes André. He likes how much André likes Isabelle. He feels comfortable, warm in his sister's kitchen.

"Was that the first time you've seen Isabelle's recent work?" André asks, topping up Paul's goblet. Paul nods.

"He thinks it's psychotic," Isabelle says, holding out her glass.

"He's not alone," André laughs, obliging her. "More people hate it than like it, that's for sure. Oh well. Nothing like a little controversy to stimulate sales."

"What do you think of it?" Paul asks André. André pours wine for himself. His face grows serious, thoughtful.

"I think if your sister only meant to stir up a little controversy, no one would pay any attention to her. But somewhere in all of that blood and guts there's a truth, a truth people respond to, whether they like it or not." They sit silently for a moment.

"It's about Mémère," Paul says.

Isabelle nods. "Cheaper than therapy. You should see my work about poor Jean-Marc."

Paul sees his sister laughing again, with her hand in the magician's box. In her forties, she can still be tricked, is happy to believe that white rabbits can be turned into white doves with a tap of the wand. She can't eat meat but has found a way to enjoy food; can't be married but has found a man like André. She sleeps peacefully at night, Isabelle, in a room with white walls and white curtains. André is probably there most nights, his arms around her. A white quilt covers them. They rest their heads on fluffy white pillows. Not a trace of gore anywhere. She leaves that locked in a room about a block away.

"She sat in that rocking chair in the kitchen," Paul begins. He wonders if he will really say it, if he will really tell. He's tearing through years of forgetting, destroying that kitchen, searching for the truth. "I was always afraid to find her in there alone. Because when no one was around, she made me come over to her. She would accuse me of hating her, and I'd have to protest, tell her no, tell her I loved her. She would pull up her dress so that I could stand closer to her, between her legs. She was old. She, she didn't smell right... She would call me her little *bonhomme*. Would kiss me on the lips and call me her little *bonhomme*, squeezing me between her legs ..."

They are silent, stunned.

Then Isabelle begins to laugh. After a moment Paul and André join in. "I can't believe it!" Isabelle gasps. "That old cunt!" She doubles over, knocking her wine glass off the table. It shatters, creating a liquid starburst on the hardwood floor.

Paul barely notices. His eyes are full of tears. He's trying to catch his breath. Laughter! Suddenly he makes a connection: *détester*, the same word in French as it is in English. No translation necessary. He is a wicked little boy again, chasing piglets around the barnyard with a willow whip. He is helping his father in the barn, pitching hay into the mangers. He is holding his mother's hand, strolling the garden and singing nursery rhymes, checking under vines for pumpkins. He is in the tree-house with Isabelle, carving dirty words into the maple's trunk with a stolen penknife. That old cunt. That old cunt.

They are soon quiet. Everything in the kitchen seems to shimmer now: the tea kettle on the stove, the overhead lamp, the doorknobs. Isabelle asks Paul what he will do if he has to leave Burkina Faso. André cleans up the mess and listens. Paul says he doesn't know. Isabelle asks him if he wants to leave the priesthood altogether. Paul says he doesn't know. She tells him that no one will care. She begins to plot and scheme, and André embellishes her ideas as they begin doing the dishes: Paul can move in with Isabelle; André has friends who are looking for someone to manage their bookstore in Place Ville-Marie; the folks will help Paul with his medical expenses until he gets on his feet …

Paul continues to sit at the table swirling his wine glass, allowing himself to be swept away by his sister's love. For some reason, it is tomorrow; and he and Isabelle are waiting outside customs to greet their parents. They will seem old to him, he knows; but he can't wait to see their faces: his father, just an aging farmer; his mother, just an aging mother. Five years. It's been five years.

Isabelle accuses Paul of being a million miles away again.

Paul smiles, says no, actually, he is not.

With Mirrors

WHEN ZASTROW says he can't pay me this time but he'll teach me a few tricks instead, I tell him sorry but I left the farm too many years ago. I tell him he'd better try one of the boys a little farther up the block. My price is my price. I ask him why it is that every john in Montreal thinks he knows some sexual act I've never seen before. It's embarrass-ing, I tell him, that they knock themselves out like that. As if they're trying to compete against all the other men I've done that day. No, I tell him, my price is my price. You want to play, you got to pay.

Zastrow says he's not talking about sex. He's talking about magic. We could make it a trade, a cultural exchange—sort of. For a weekly tumble at his studio, he will teach me how to fuck with people's minds. Don't I ever get tired of just plain fucking? I ask him for a cigarette. Magic? Turning silk handkerchiefs into white doves? Sawing beautiful ladies in half? Zastrow snaps his fingers and a business card appears. He says to give him a call if I change my mind. Don't hold your breath, I say. But I know I'll call. I'm such a sucker for that kind of crap: pink-eyed rabbits being pulled out of hats, people vanishing into thin air. He turns away, with a flap of his stupid black cape. He disappears into the mist, leaving me alone on Ste-Catherine. Zastrow the Great, Master of Illusions and Legerdemain. That's what his card says.

I wouldn't call Zastrow a regular. Regulars generally have kinks, want a certain type of boy because he looks a little like their brother, their army sergeant, their childhood buddy. That's not Zastrow. As I recall, he's pretty much by-the-book in the sack. A little too touchy-feely, maybe. My regulars, especially the Canucks, like me because I'm blond and hairless and American—exotic for Quebec. And though I look like the perfect little angel, I can be pretty rough. I'm as close as most of them will ever come to being abused by a Malibu beach boy.

But Zastrow doesn't exactly fall into the category of Anonymous John, either. For one thing, I've been with him a half-dozen times. For another, I know his name. Generally, the ones I call Anonymous John are married and in their thirties, guys who feel guilty about liking boys. That's why they insist on a new face every time. As if by doing me more than once they risk being recognized while they're out shopping with their children at Place Bonaventure. As if I ever go shopping at Place Bonaventure.

Frankly, I'm not really sure what Zastrow's deal is. Whenever I'm out working the bars, he always nods hello, even if he's with a date. He's not ugly or deformed. He only wears the cape when he has a gig, and he has a decent-sized dick. Okay, so he coughs a little. But that's what condoms are for. And if he were a freak—if he cut boys up—we'd all know about him by now. It's the worst thing of all, I'm afraid; the one thing I cannot tolerate. I'm afraid he actually thinks he likes me.

—Of course Ricky isn't my real name.
—Well then, what is your real name?
—For chrissake, what difference does that make?
—Tell me. I want to know.
—Okay, whatever. It's Scotty.
—So why do they call you Ricky?
—Because when I started on Ste-Catherine, there was already a Scott. There weren't any Rickys yet. And I didn't see the point in changing back, after some freak killed the other Scott by hanging him from the heating pipes. I had regular clients by then.
—It didn't scare you, what happened to this other Scott?
—His name wasn't really Scott. It was Charlie. You just don't think about it. It's what you call an occupational hazard.

—So what's your last name?

—Jesus! Leave me alone.

—What's the big secret? Tell me your last name.

—Leave me the fuck alone, man.

Zastrow says the illusionist business isn't what it used to be. It's 1984, positively Orwellian out there. Entire ways of life and segments of the population are disappearing into thin air. Plus if people want to feel hoodwinked, he says, all they got to do is turn on the nightly news. They can watch their tax dollars disappear into the pockets of MPs before their very eyes. Poof! Sorry! Gone without a trace.

We're at his studio, down in Old Montreal. If I'd known he had a whole frigging warehouse, I'd've never agreed to this deal. Or I'd've at least insisted on cab fare. Before now, Zastrow and I have always gone back to my room at the Valmont Hotel—where I take most of my drive-up johns, unless it's just a blow job, in which case I do them in their cars. Zastrow doesn't have a car, of course. He prowls Ste-Catherine on foot, my only walk-up client.

One good look around is enough to tell me where all his money goes. Besides a big bed over in the corner—which is actually kind of cool, because it's under a skylight and surrounded by real palm trees growing out of a half-dozen old toilets—the place is stuffed full of magic: wire pens of doves and rabbits; giant lacquer boxes with arm and leg holes cut out of them; metal hoops and colourful plastic rings dangling from hooks on walls; a couple of trunks brimming with spangly clothes; one of those antique crushed-velvet lounging sofas; a pile of naked mannequin limbs and torsos. And he has mirrors everywhere, dozens of them. Some that give crazy, distorted reflections, some that stand as tall as me, some suspended from the ceiling.

Zastrow asks me if I had a hard time finding the place. No, I tell him, but it was a bitch getting here because my last john practically lived in LaSalle. I tell him I nearly froze my ass off waiting for the bus. He reaches over and puts his arms around me, says he'll fix that right up. I push him away. I say no offense, but business is business. Magic first, then dick.

***

—Look at this one. His eyes are white.

—Do you like rabbits, Scotty?

—Yeah, they're okay. We used to have a bunch of them back in Vermont, where I grew up. I'd take them out of the hutch every once in a while, you know, to pet them. They like to be scratched between the ears, see?

—Rabbits don't make very good pets though, do they? They're not very bright.

—Wouldn't know. My father raised them to eat.

—Didn't your parents let you have pets?

—Just my father. My mother's dead.

—I'm sorry.

—You're always saying that, man. As if everything's your fault. It bugs me.

—I'll try to remember that, Scotty.

—So what were we talking about?

—Pets.

—I had a pony, once. A Shetland. Actually, it wasn't really my pony. Our neighbours just boarded it in our barn. Her name was Pegasus and she was mean as hell. The neighbour's kids never came over to ride her because she nipped. But I made friends with her. I brought her an apple every day one summer until she let me ride her.

—Whatever happened to Pegasus?

—Oh, nothing. One night my father and some of the boys got drunk, tried to have a little rodeo. They were too heavy for her and she broke a leg. The old man had to put her down the next morning. Lied about it, told the neighbours I tried to make her jump.

—I'm very sorry.

—There you go again. It was just a pony. And she wasn't even mine.

When you open the box, it looks like it's painted completely black on the inside. But only a couple of the walls are really black. The rest are mirrors. After you put a rabbit in and shut the door, you wave a wand around the top and say a whole lot of nonsense. That distracts the audience's attention away from the fact you're working a lever in the back with the other hand. The lever repositions the mirrors inside, so that when you finally tap on the top of box and open up the door, it looks like the rabbit has disappeared. But it really hasn't. The mirrors are just reflecting blackness and not rabbit.

That was the first trick Zastrow showed me. In the last month or so I've learned all sorts of other ones. A dozen card tricks, the secret to pouring milk out of a pitcher into a paper cone, how to join and unjoin metal rings. This week, I'm working on making the magic wand dance in the air. Zastrow keeps laughing, every time I get caught up in the fishing wire. I tell him to eat shit, but I have to laugh myself. A couple of times he's had to stop cooking to untangle me. This fuck-for-a-trick thing has stretched itself into a trick, a fuck and supper. I'm not complaining. It beats freezing my ass off over on Ste-Catherine. And he's a pretty good cook.

Tonight when we sit down to eat, he has a new proposition for me. He's working up a deal with one of the gay bars in the Village for a magic show at their New Year's Eve party. He says they'll only go for it if it's sexy. Normally, he works with this UQAM kid named Céline. He saws her in half, sticks knives through her, makes her appear out of a basket dressed like a harem girl during his snake-charmer routine. He says she's a knockout, a real professional, but she's not going to fly at this party of nasty French queens—except as comic relief. His idea is to start with Céline, doing a couple of standard tricks to warm them up. He'll teach her some raunchy fag jokes, to keep things moving along. Then he'll put her in the snake basket, make her vanish and—Abracadabra!— have me pop out instead, wearing a g-string and turban. I'll do a little bump and grind and the queens will go wild. He says we can end with an erotic disco version of the wand dance, if I get good enough. What do I think?

I tell him he's got a screw loose. No, he says, he's serious; I'm actually getting to be a pretty good magician—how about ten per cent of the take? I tell him it'll be my dick bouncing around up there, bringing in the Elizabeths. I won't even consider it for less than twenty-five. He says he can't do it. He says most of the take has to go toward rent or he'll be out on his ass. The best he can do is fifteen per cent. Couldn't I consider it a personal favour to him, a gesture of friendship? I say twenty. He says deal.

    —What I like's not really the point, is it Zastrow?
    —I'm serious. What turns you on? Just between you and me. There's no one else to hear, none of your Valmont Hotel buddies to laugh at you. All the rules are suspended. What could I do—do for you—that would really get you off?
    —I get off every time. That's why they keep coming back.
    —It's not about your cock. What I'm talking about happens deeper inside; in your stomach, in your head.
    —For me, sex is strictly about my cock. The tool of the trade.
    —Come on, play along. What's the harm? Tell me the one thing I could do to really excite you.
    —I don't think you're that good a magician, man.
    —What do you mean?
    —I doubt you can turn yourself into a girl.

When I finally get to Zastrow's today, Céline is there. I have a key now, so I let myself in. She's as beautiful as he said, floating above that crushed-velvet lounging sofa, chatting with him in French as he waves his wand over her body to prove it isn't done with wires. They're talking about college stuff, courses they've both taken. Laughing. It's like a real spell, and I don't want to break it.

I wander over when they finally notice me. I ask Zastrow in French what it's going to be today—more wand dancing? I can tell he's impressed. He introduces me to Céline. He says I'll have to work out the final steps of the wand dance on my own. That disappoints me a little. I've gotten pretty fired up about it, now that I've found some club music that'll work. But he says we need to get started on the basket illusion. That's why Céline's there.

It turns out to be pretty complicated—especially with the turban on—and I keep messing up. I can tell I'm making Zastrow mad. He hasn't been feeling well again, and he sighs each time we have to take it from the top. Céline tries to keep everything light by cracking jokes and patting us both on the back. But he eventually blows up at me. If

I weren't so goddamn stupid, he says, we could make a little progress. He says it's like trying to train one of his no-mind rabbits to sit still in the black box. I tell him to eat shit. I tell him I don't need his two-bit, fleabag magic tricks. I say I got better things to do. He throws up his hands. God forbid he should keep me from plying the tools of my trade, he says.

Céline clears her throat. She mentions, real quiet, how she can see we've all had enough for one day. Picking up her things, she tells us she's got to get over to the McGill library where she's meeting her boyfriend, a med student there. She puts her coat on and heads for the door. She turns, though, and gives me a smile. She says in French that she hopes she'll see me next week—since we've got some work ahead of us. Zastrow follows her out to set up a time. To talk about me behind my back, no doubt. I lie down on the crushed-velvet sofa and cover my eyes with my hand. I have a headache.

When Zastrow gets back, he asks me what I'm still doing here. I tell him business is business; I owe him a fuck. He stares down at me, ruffles my hair and says not today. He doesn't feel up to it. How about if I help him with another little project he's working on? I ask him if it's a new trick for the act. He says he's not sure; it might be, if it works. He says we'll have to wait and see, which is fine by me. I don't really feel like hitting the streets yet.

We clear a space over by the big windows. He has me draw a chalk box on the floor, three meters square. He places a folding chair in the center of it. For the rest of the afternoon, we position mirrors around the square. At first we don't say much, but then we start to talk. He asks me all sorts of personal questions. And I answer most of them—I don't know why—while we work, hanging and moving mirrors. I hint a couple of times that I'm getting hungry, but Zastrow's mind isn't on food, plus I know he's short on cash. Finally, I run down the block and get some Chinese for us. He's sitting in the folding chair when I get back, smoking and staring off into space, reflected over and over again in the mirrors. I've seen it before, that look. He hasn't got a whole lot longer. I hold up the food and he smiles. Thanks Scotty, he says.

***

—She died when I was four years old. I hardly remember her at all.

—How did she die?

—Car accident. She slid off a bridge during a snow storm and drowned.

—That's pretty horrible. Your father must have been devastated.

—He took to the bottle pretty heavy.

—He never remarried?

—Didn't have to. He got along just fine on me.

We do have a hell of a lot of fun together, the three of us. And we're getting good. Every time I leap out of the basket and start shaking my hips, Céline bursts into a fit of giggles under Zastrow's cape. She says she can't help it; I look too goddamn cute. She says my wand dance finale makes her hot, even though she's seen it a hundred times. I can tell Zastrow is pleased with how everything's going, though he doesn't ever say much. Lately he has to sit down to catch his breath. He keeps telling us it's the tail end of the flu. We both know better. We just tell him to get it checked out before the club date. It would really suck if we had to cancel it. It's going to be a good show.

Lately, after practice, Céline has been staying for spaghetti. Zastrow calls it the beggar's banquet. Sometimes she brings a bottle of cheap Chianti and we get a little drunk off it. Zastrow tells us about his past loves, which are many: the sailor, the Ice Follies star, the cowboy from Alberta, the concert pianist. Céline tells him he's still good-looking, which isn't true at all these days. She asks him why he doesn't find himself a stable college professor. Zastrow shrugs and smiles at me. He says who has the time with so many business obligations to tend to?

Céline tells us about her boyfriend. She confesses that even though he's really handsome; he's lousy in bed. She wonders if it's ever occurred to him that women like to have orgasms, too. She says he's from a good family, an Anglo one, and his parents put up with her well enough. They don't speak French, don't know about the magic. She tells me if she weren't so broke from Christmas presents, she'd buy up a whole week of my time. A whole week of orgasms.

Zastrow winks at me and says to her, with the economy the way it is, I might consider running a holiday special. I ask for more wine. Céline tells me I'm blushing.

I can't remember the last time Zastrow and I actually did it. When we aren't rehearsing with Céline, I sit inside the chalk line and talk to him while he rearranges the mirrors. He says he's been thinking about how to do this for months. Now that I see what he's after, I've kind of lost interest. There's a little white-eyed rabbit I like. I hold him in my lap and pet him. Around midnight, he calls me a cab. He goes to bed. I hit the streets.

Most spaghetti nights I tell them funny stories about Anonymous John. But tonight I tell them about the farm, about the good old days, when my Aunt Gloria was living with us after my Mom died, just before she got married and moved to Boston. I tell them about the time the three of us bundled up to cut down a Christmas tree. We headed off into the woodlot behind the barn, with me riding in the toboggan. It took us forever to choose a tree. Gloria finally decided on the top half of a blue spruce. She climbed onto my Dad's shoulders to reach the spot where she wanted to cut. I yelled timber when it fell. We sang "Jingle Bells" and "Joy To the World" on the walk back to the house, the tree roped to the toboggan. Too bad it's all bullshit.

Céline proposes a toast to good food and good friends. We clink glasses. After she leaves, Zastrow fiddles with the mirrors while I sit in the chair. Neither one of us is in the mood to talk. Maybe an hour goes by. Then, suddenly, he stands back and says it's done. What's done? I ask, looking up. He has a huge smile on his face. We switch places and I see that he's right, it works. But it's kind of creepy: dead silence except for the wind; all those mirrors shivering in the draft.

He jumps up and gives me a hug. He laughs, a strange musical laugh, before he starts to cough. I whisper into his shoulder: can I stay over? He whispers back: yes.

—She'd never touch me; not after where I've been.
—Are you afraid of where you've been, Scotty?
—We've talked about this already. I'm not afraid of dying. In my line of work you can't be.

34

—Well I'm terrified of it. I'm afraid there's nothing afterward. What if it really is all over, the minute you stop breathing. Not a trick, not an illusion.

—So what's so great about breathing?

—You know about me, don't you? I'm sorry. I should have told you up front.

—Forget about it. That's what condoms are for, right?

—But the only safe sex is no sex.

—Occupational hazard.

We don't have practice this week because it's Christmas. Céline is at home with her family, her boyfriend. I call Zastrow from the lobby pay phone at the Valmont. I ask him if he wants to run through my parts with me. I'm a little nervous about going on stage next week. But he says no. He sounds terrible. I ask him if he wants me to bring him something; some soup maybe, or some Chinese food. He says no, he isn't keeping anything down. I hang up the phone and hail a cab.

I find Zastrow lying in bed, in among the palm trees, staring up at the blue, blue sky. I go and get my rabbit, crawl under the covers beside him. The sheets are soaked. I tell him he should really check himself into a hospital. He tells me he doesn't want to go that way, with tubes stuck up his nose and ass. He's had his good spells and his bad spells over the last couple of years. This is a bad one, the last one. He has decided to gobble a fistful of pills, if I'll wait with him. He wants me to promise I'll go over to the clinic and get tested. I stroke his head and tell him I get tested once a month. What does he think, that I just left the farm?

He says I should take anything I want from the place, before the bill collectors come. I ask him what his real name is. He tells me it's Max. Maximilian Zastrow. I ask him about his family. He talks about growing up in Toronto until he gets too confused. Then he apologizes some more about not being able to make it to the show. He says it would have been a terrific way to bring in 1985. I tell him I think so, too. He says he'll miss our little chats. I tell him I will, too. He says I have a talent, a real talent for magic.

When it's over, I get up and put the rabbit back in his cage. I cross the studio, past the mannequin parts, past the hoops and rings, past the lacquer boxes. I cross the chalk mark on the floor and sit in the folding chair. I don't know how long I'll sit here, reflecting the blue, blue sky and not Scotty. I can't think about it right now. Because even though it's all done with mirrors, I feel a little better, bombarded by this white light and heat, knowing I've disappeared.

Lurid, Psychotic Colours

HE ASKED IN APPALLING Dutch if he could share my table. I said suit yourself in English, found my place on the page and carried on reading. He sat opposite me and took out a book of his own. After a moment, he asked in English why this café seemed so particularly busy. Canadian was my guess. Too much music in the voice for the States. I shrugged. Cafés are cafés, I said; sometimes they're busy, especially in the summer, especially on the Prinsengracht. No further questions. A man went whizzing by on an Opa bike, then a delivery van, then two women deep in conversation.

When Martijn came round, the Canadian ordered a peppermint tea. He asked me if I needed anything. I hate people like that. Need anything. I am perfectly capable of ordering for myself. I told Martijn, in Dutch, that I was all right. I said I was leaving anyway, in a minute or two.

—Your English is excellent.
—I'm not Dutch.
—Then your Dutch is excellent.
—And?
—So what are you reading?
—Absolute crap. Now even lawyers think they're novelists.
—I'm from Quebec originally. But now I'm living in London, working as a trader. I'm here on holiday. How about you?
—I really must be going …

—I'm bothering you. Sorry. I guess I'm a little lonely. Back home, people sometimes go to cafés to talk. Sorry. I'll be quiet; it's your table.

I waited for him to wish me have-a-nice-day and leave. He didn't.

Martijn came back with his peppermint tea. It smelled lovely, like village life somewhere humble. I ordered one for myself. I know, I know: I'm hopeless. I guess *I'm* a little lonely. I can't resist anyone who tells the truth.

I told this Canadian I worked in The Hague as a freelance interpreter; a long commute, yes, but necessary. Because any foreigner living in Holland, I told him, could only seriously consider living in Amsterdam. He accepted this as fact without comment. Another Opa bike. He asked where in England I was from. I told him from the Isle of Man. A beat of silence. I said, you know, Isle of Man, where the Manx cat is from? He wasn't good at geography, he said, or accents. What did that make me?

Charlotte, I told him. I'm Charlotte.

He said his name was Guy. And the way he said it rhymed with me.

I have never been to the Isle of Man. I've heard it's just some boring, characterless place where rich men keep post boxes for complicated tax reasons. But oh the metaphoric possibilities of that name! I read quite a lot, you see. I like to read about islands. And so I prefer to picture the Isle of Man to be more like Easter Island: littered with huge stone heads having phalluses for noses and recessed shadows for eyes, vacant eyes that stare out at the sea—at nothing. An island full of stone-cold, immobile men. Englishmen. My father.

I've said that my father was a sheep farmer on the Isle of Man. I've described him as someone of few words, a war hero, a dedicated family man, a labourer of ancient and worn hands. I've described his landscapes as damp stone and stinging nettles, as relentless wind smelling of peat fire. I've described misty forests, jagged cliff sides, half-hearted suns giving no warmth. The Isle of Man is a brutal place, I've said. Cats have no tails there. But I have no idea, really.

We—the Canadian and I—sipped our teas. The late afternoon sun was on our faces. We were running out of chit-chat. A canal boat full of tourists churned by. Over the loudspeaker, a guide pointed out the Anne Frank house on the right, *sur la droite, zum Rechts, a la derecha*. She didn't bother with Dutch. I asked the Canadian what sights he'd visited so far. He said he'd been to the Rijks Museum, the Anne Frank House, the Rembrandtsplein. He admitted he'd even strolled through the Red Light District the evening before, just to say he'd done it.

—And what did you think?

—I find Amsterdam a little sinister. I've been to New York and Miami. Montreal, of course. They all have rough parts of town, but I never felt as nervous as last night.

—That's because in America the danger is The Other, which is easily avoided. You just have to know where not to wander. But here in Amsterdam, I'd say the danger is The Self: what your secret self will do without limits or guidelines.

—Maybe so. But sometimes our limitations are set for us, Charlotte.

Stunning silence. I ground my coffee cup in half-turns round its saucer. He quickly added that he was talking about himself, of course. A half-dozen more excruciating revolutions. Panicked, he said he planned to visit the Van Gogh museum the next morning. Had I ever been? Then: Oh, perhaps not … yet another verbal blush. This time I decided to let him off the hook. No, I said, I'd never been, though its collection often cropped up in conversation. Tell me, I said, just what is so great about Van Gogh? He considered my question carefully before answering. All the lurid, psychotic colours, he said. Layers of paint so thick that some of the canvases are still not dry. Landscapes, he said, where the skies are heaving and thrashing; still lifes where cane chairs creep tentatively out from corners; bouquets where the irises and sunflowers scream Look at me! Look at me! Self-portraits where the eyes of stony-faced, ginger-haired men follow you round the room.

Oh, I said.

Would I care to join him? We could meet here tomorrow morning, at the café, and walk over together. Martijn came round again. I said I really must be going—a few errands to run before work. Was I going to The Hague this late in the day? he asked. Oh you know how diplomats are, I said. To change the subject, I asked him which hotel he was at. He said it was nothing fancy; a small pension just off the Leidseplein. I offered to walk him home, since it was on my way. He said he'd like that. He insisted on paying the bill.

I could tell, out on the pavement, that he wanted to take my arm. I've developed a sixth sense about this. I can feel their hands hovering, just above my shoulder blade. People are always trying to protect poor, defenseless Charlotte. I told him to follow me. I set the pace. I could hear him chuckling behind me.

—Bloody Yank. What are you laughing at?

—Watch your step. Dog doo at eleven o'clock. I'm laughing because you said "home" back there. That you'd walk me home. The ex-junkie born-again hippie at the front desk of my hotel doesn't exactly remind me of my father.

—Exactly why people come to Amsterdam.

—What is?

—Because they would never find their parents here.

—Pretty different from the Isle of Man, I bet.

—Wait, I want to show you something.

I pointed out a small wooden door on the right, a half-step down from street level. I told him to lift up on the wrought iron latch and push hard. He did. I told him the passage was public, he should follow the small cobbled walkway to the end, I was right behind him. Was I sure it was all right? There are no private spaces in Amsterdam, I whispered, only secret ones. I prodded him in the back.

He gasped when he entered the garden at the end. (How could he not tell it was coming? Could he not smell the plants and the earth and the mold?) We sat on one of the stone benches on the sunnier side and listened to the birds. Rooks, mostly. The odd mourning dove. Pigeons. He said he hadn't seen such a beautiful, quiet place in a very long time. It was my turn to accept what he said as fact. I haven't much use for adjectives like beautiful. Or ugly.

I asked him to describe Quebec. He didn't describe anything, of course. No one ever does. He just talked about his life. He said his parents were dairy farmers. They also made maple syrup in the spring. Steam is sweet in a sugarhouse, he said. It takes three hours to boil thirty gallons of maple sap into one gallon of fancy grade syrup. The steam is sticky. It clings to you. When you wake up in the morning, after a day of sugaring, you can smell it on your pillow.

He slipped his hand into mine. It seemed a perfectly natural thing for him to do. Sugar houses. Sticky maple cauls like cobwebs clinging to faces. I didn't take my hand away. I didn't tell him about the bathhouse, how the odour of disinfectant lingers on my jumper long after I leave, how I gag on it all the way home—on the tram, in the lift, in the hallway outside my flat.

I told him I really must be going. I stood. I hoped standing would somehow release my hand from his. It didn't. He simply stood as well, to catch himself up with our hands. And he took my arm in the cobbled alley. We made our way back out to the Prinsengracht side by side.

I am not, of course, a diplomatic translator in The Hague. I work at a gay bathhouse in the Red Light District. I sit in a glass booth at the entrance and collect the money through a little hole cut out of the front. The owners, two Kuwaiti brothers, hired me because they thought I would lend the establishment the impression of discretion. But I do speak several languages. That part is true. It's mostly a listening skill. Not that it makes much of a difference at the bathhouse. The customers hand me their twenty euros. Only a few of them venture the odd, nervous observation about the rain. Their voices tell stories about their lives, though: German businessmen with young children waiting up for a night-night call before trundling off to bed; pissed-as-bastards London lads daring each other to be naughty, but secretly curious beyond words; elderly Dutch gentlemen seeing nothing wrong with paying for sex now that they've lost their looks.

I take their money without comment.

The stench! Nothing reeks, I've decided, like wet, hot body hair or stale semen. Except the industrial disinfectant the owners use to cover it all over. The impression of cleanliness. Imagine trying to get aroused in such a place! Disinfectant is to pine forest what bathhouse must be to sex.

Obviously, I've never seen the goings on behind my little glass booth. I'm told the men take all their clothes off and hang them neatly in cupboards in the changing room. Then they disappear, noiselessly, naked, into the unlit steam room. There are two types, I'm told. The first type of man makes his way immediately to the back, where there are wooden benches. He is called a *kip*, a hen. The second type roams around, finding his way by touch, groping for what he likes, for what he wants. He is called a *haan*, a rooster. No one can see anything. It's all attraction based only on texture or taste or talk. Who knows why I work there. I have to eat, I guess.

We stopped, midway up a busy pavement off the Leidseplein. We were apparently at his hotel. Suddenly, he began digging a jangly set of keys out of his backpack. Oh dear, I thought, it's going to be one of those horrible places where students or stag-party bachelors stay— above an Indonesian restaurant, it would seem—announced only by a cracked wooden door. He invited me up to the lounge. I thought: what on earth for? I said: only for a moment. I was already ten minutes late for work.

— Um, Charlotte, I wouldn't expect anything like a beautiful garden with stone benches at the top of this staircase, by the way.
—Just as long as there aren't people shooting up on the sofa.
—Oh, well, in that case, maybe we'd better go to your place.
—How can you possibly sleep in a place smelling constantly of curry? Doesn't it make you hungry?
—I'm always hungry.

The lounge had the feel of someplace that didn't get much light. Sandalwood incense did not help the mustiness, just added to the unpleasantness. The sofa was a cool moist vinyl with cracks that pinched at my legs when I sat down. He told me he'd be right back, then disappeared up another staircase. Over the din of pots and pans, I could hear someone (the ex-junkie born-again manager?) arguing on the phone with the PTT. Of course he'd paid last month's bill, it was outrageous how the mailman kept losing his payments, there must be some conspiracy, where did his tax money go, anyway? I wondered about fleas. Then the thump of Guy's boots on the staircase. When he sat next to me, we both slid into each other, our hips colliding. No apologies. He'd brought a bar of chocolate from his room. He broke it and handed me half.

The Abenaki, a tribe of the Algonquian nation, taught French settlers how to collect and boil maple sap. This process, Guy informed me, is called sugaring. It happens only one week a year, after the first spring thaw, when Guy's father and granddad slosh through the mud in their Wellies and hang galvanized tin buckets from wooden spigots on all the maples trees. These spigots, apparently, they tap into the trunks with wooden mallets. Some of the larger trees hold as many as six or eight buckets, have spigot scars like the arms of heroin addicts. Then the waiting begins, waiting for the last blizzard of the season. This final cold snap causes clear maple sap to drip from the spigots into the buckets. When the sap is running, Guy's granddad and father take a sledge out to the maple stand, pulled by two workhorses named Molly and Dan. The sledge has a huge galvanized tank mounted on it. Brimming buckets are emptied into the tub and rehung. When full, the tub is hauled back to the sugarhouse for boiling.

Guy said he was talking too much. Nervous, he guessed. He asked me about my family—what were they like? I said there wasn't much to tell. I found it difficult to concentrate, what with that man screaming in Dutch at the phone company. And there wasn't nearly enough chocolate to last the conversation out. I told him I was the first and only child, my mother having died of complications during my birth. My father had done his best to raise me, to be sure, but working at the shop all day and then washing my nappies at night had got to be too much for him. So my auntie had taken me in.

***

—Shop? What shop? Didn't you say your father was a sheep farmer on the Isle of Man?

—He was, after he gave me up. Before that, we lived with his people on the Isle of Skye. I joined him on the farm a few years later. He sent for me.

—Oh. What kind of store did he run on the Isle of Skye?

—My father was a butcher.

When Guy's lips touched mine I wasn't surprised. His kisses tasted sweet. Not like the bar of chocolate we'd been eating. More like the inside of a sweet person. And his face felt smoother than I remembered a man's to be. It didn't feel as though he had a beard. So this was a different man. An entirely different man. A face without those textures and curves. Not my father at all.

I stood up. He asked me what was wrong. I told him I didn't like it there, in that damp smelly hotel. Sorry, he said; should he walk me to the train station? No, I said. I felt dizzy, a little disorientated. I'm not going to The Hague, I said; I'm going back to my flat. He didn't respond. One thousand one, one thousand two, one thousand three. I'm not a mind reader. Well, I said. Are you coming or not?

The Isle of Skye. No, I've never been there, either. It's supposed to be lovely—yet another empty English word, lovely. With charming views of the sea and quaint villages nestled among sheep-dotted hillsides. Charming. Quaint. Nothing lovely about the smell of sheep in my mind. Especially wet, Scottish ones. But there you go.

When I'm working at the bathhouse, I try to imagine it, The Isle of Skye. Anything to take my mind off from the hush in those damp rooms behind me. But all I can conjure are islands I've read about off the Mosquito Coast, tiny islands with something called cloud forests. On my Isle of Skye, there are craggy peaks so steep the rainforests draping them poke above the cloud cover. I imagine the strong smell of rain, sweet moisture condensing on my skin, not yet liquid, too cool for steam, somewhere in between states of matter: clouds. On my Isle of Skye, you can climb strangler fig vines like ladders to the very top of the forest canopy. From there you can stroll gigantic interwoven mahogany and ebony branches for miles. You can glimpse rare and exotic creatures among the wisps of cloud: scarlet macaws, ocelots, howler monkeys, toucans, two-toed sloths. Every once in a while you can stumble upon a break in the foliage, and from there you can see the rest of the known world in all its colours: emerald, azure, scarlet, gold.

Imagine a steamy, quiet place above the earth—an island above an island. A place where there is only you, where there are no men to damage or destroy things with their spades and cleavers, no men to come to you in the middle of the night with whiskey on their breaths, no men to whisper to you that you are lovely, that you are beautiful, that you are charming, that they are lonely. Oh, imagine a place where there are only sky-borne creatures so rare they almost never come into contact with human females, don't know enough about them to be afraid.

I barely remember the tram ride back to my flat. We stood the whole way—there were no seats—and swayed together. I said I felt tired. Guy lay my forehead against the front of his jacket. Time went by. My mind filled up with hunting trips in deep pine forests, probably dozens of them, quiet evenings crouched before wood fires, long walks with the family dog. We nearly missed my stop. We tried chatting. But I couldn't follow the thread of conversation. I realized I'd never been in the lift of my building with another person. It suddenly seemed small, Guy suddenly seemed so big. He said he liked my flat. I offered to make us tea. He said: you don't really work in The Hague do you? I put my fingers to his face to find his lips. Then I put my mouth there. The kettle whistled and whistled.

It wasn't what I expected at all. Nothing to endure. I kept waiting for the moment when I would have to clench my fists and say, Right, here we go, this is it. But it grew dark outside my bedroom window (I have as many names for shades of darkness as an Eskimo for snow), then it grew light again. It was rather how I imagined making love to another woman might be, a bit timid, a shared language: both wanting the same things, both sensing by taste and texture what might please the other. Loads of doing nothing at all, really. Breathing with the same rhythm. Talking.

He told me his gran would come into the sugarhouse in the morning, after his father and granddad had been boiling all night. She would balance two stacked cookie sheets of donut dough, waiter-style, on one hand. (What, do you suppose, is a cookie sheet?) In the other, there'd be a pot of coffee. In the pockets of her apron, a half-dozen eggs. First she'd pour each of the men a cup of strong black coffee. Then she'd fry up the donuts in the boiling sap. Then she'd crack the eggs one by one on the edge of the vat and poach them alongside the donuts. Everything would be caramelized by the time she'd scoop it out with a slotted spoon. Breakfast.

He asked me if I missed home. I shrugged. I told him this was home, waving my hand round the room—wherever I was at the moment. I told him I had wandered the world in books since I'd left the Isle of Wight, learning languages, absorbing cultures, looking for I don't know what. You mean the Isle of Skye, he prompted—wasn't that what I had said? He kissed my neck and told me it was okay, I didn't have to talk about the past if I didn't feel like it. We could just lie there. I told him I didn't have much use for the past. But I said thank you.

I am from the Isle of Wight, Guy. A completely unremarkable place, popular with working-class England on holiday. Bog-standard coastal town, nothing fancy. It smells of the sea and of box hedges. I want you to know, I can well imagine white: crisp sheets snapping on the line, freshly starched aprons on all the waitresses, the sun darting in and out of harmless clouds. A perfect place for virgins, really.

White is the utter absence of colour, what most people see with their eyes closed.

My parents ran a guesthouse on the Isle of Wight. And after my father ran off, my mother began sleeping with some of the clientele to make ends meet. She did this cheerfully. She was a cheerful sort of person.

My father disappeared when I was very young. My mother maintains he was lost at sea. She's still there, on the Isle of Wight Lies. But one of my mean-spirited cousins told me my father went up to London to be gay. Silly cow. Once, just before coming to

Amsterdam, this cousin invited me to tea. She was meant to talk me out of going away. How would I ever manage by myself? As if I hadn't spent my entire life in isolation. She told me my father used to corner her in the loo at family gatherings, ask her to take her pants off and give them to him, ask her if he could kiss her, all the while trying to insert his finger up her bottom. I said it didn't sound very much like he was gay to me. But it all made sense, she said, why else would he only be attracted to little girls with boyish bodies?

Nothing makes any sense.

Once, Guy, at the bathhouse, I was collecting a customer's entry fee. This man commented on what a lovely face he thought I had— he was English—and his voice told a terrible story. It caressed my eyelids and whispered, Never mind, never mind. It asked if I wanted to ride on his shoulders. It promised to send me books from faraway islands and exotic cities. It was the voice of a war hero, a dedicated family man, a labourer of ancient and worn hands. I thought I might suffocate in that little booth. Or scream and not be able to stop. But I took his money and said thank you. And he slipped silently inside. *Kip* or *haan*? I thought. And I worried this one all the way home: Rooster or hen?

We lay there not talking on the island of my bed, the French windows open, the sweat drying on our skin. It was the first time ever that my flat didn't smell entirely of me. Sweet sweat, from a sugary smelling man. Not at all the same sweat as at the bathhouse. (How could it be sex—what those men do there—now that I know? How could it be sex unless the scent, the smell, of your lover lingers on your fingertips afterward, lingers on your pillow? How could it be sex if after you leave the place, you smell of industrial pine forest?)

Canal boats churned past. Laughter in the street below. I asked Guy why he would go to the trouble of seducing a blind woman. There must be easier shags in Amsterdam, I said. He laughed. He said he was extremely ugly, almost frightening to look at. Apparently, when he was a boy, he'd got into an argument with his brother. They were in the sugarhouse. It was spring, boiling time. Their father had stepped outside for a piss. His brother had dunked his face in the heaving, boiling vat.

I thought about my empty glass booth. I knew I wouldn't turn up for work that evening, either. I knew, in fact, that I would never go back to the bathhouse, not even to collect what they owed me in wages. The owners won't care very much; people disappear all the time in Amsterdam. No. First I would take a long bath. Then I would go out for breakfast with Guy, for pancakes with maple syrup at an American café across the road. And after that, I would go with Guy to the Van Gogh Museum. Because more than anything, I wanted to see the lurid psychotic colours, see the heaving and bursting skies. Stare back at stony-faced, ginger-haired men with eyes that follow you round the room.

Castaway

Two MEN ARE SEATED third row center of an empty concert hall.

Stefan sips cold coffee, wondering why they always look like the evil stepsisters of cellists. Where are the women of the publicity photos, he laments, the ones who drape themselves, pouting, over their instruments? He takes a bite of cold pastrami on rye.

Eric hands Stefan the next CV. This one has a bit more promise, he says. Julliard. One of Helmerson's protégés. Rostropovich Prize, 1996. Featured by half the chamber orchestras of North America while she was still in braces.

Stefan sigh and nods, reminds himself to tell the girl to get him tuna fish next time.

Ready when you are, Eric shouts into the void.

She peers out from the wings. Maybe they're not as ferocious as everyone says. She tugs at her top, wishing she had worn the white blouse instead. Her mother insisted on this clingy black purchase, quoting from one of her cable shows that plunging necklines are slimming. She decides the blond man looks nicer than the fat one eating the sandwich. She'll play to the blond one.

She places her hands on either side of her Gagliano's waist and lifts it to her face. She presses her lips to its left F hole and whispers, I love you. Into the right she whispers, I need you.

She strides over to what seems like an impossibly small wooden chair center stage. She lowers herself onto it, testing its sturdiness before positioning the cello between her legs. She resists the urge to tug at the back of her top again by poising her bow over the D string.

Isn't that a Gagliano? Eric says.
    Hands like hams, Stefan thinks.
    Haydn's Cello Concerto in D Major, she says.
    Now there's a surprise, Stefan hisses to Eric.
    Eric signals for her to begin.
    She closes her eyes.
    She begins.

She is marooned on an island off the Mosquito Coast. There are no other survivors—not even her mother—of the ill-fated cruise ship that finally hired her as first-and-only cello for its Vegas-style Broadway revue. She alone has drifted to safety atop her faithful Gagliano.

    She manages nicely on bananas, coconuts, and dates.
    In fact, the rigours of island life have quickly melted away those extra pounds. Her hair is now sun-bleached, her skin bronzed, her stomach taut, her breasts and buttocks perky. Her work uniform—a black clingy top with matching black trousers—has long since fallen away in tattered ribbons.

    She makes for her favourite waterfall.
    It's on the remotest part of the island, in a hidden cleft of volcanic rock surrounded by rare orchids with callas cascading all around. First she must cross a beach where thousands of vermilion ghost crabs scuttle drunkenly with the ebb and flow of tides. Then she must traverse a glade of plane trees, keeping an eye out for wild boars that stun unsuspecting prey with their overwhelming stench before tearing into the flesh with long yellowed fangs. Next she must swing Tarzan-style over a clicking river of army ants that leaves only a swath of bare earth behind. Finally she hears the hush of rainwater on rock. She parts the palm fronds and there it is.

    The gentle spray, when she steps beneath it, is the same temperature as her body. She relaxes under its insistent pulse. The most delicious moment of her day: eyes closed, head bowed, arms crossed over her breasts. Hugging. Waiting.

She knows the stranger is watching—the island's only other inhabitant—deciding when to emerge from the ferns. She nods, eyes closed, in anticipation of his arrival. She hears the pop of each button, the unzip of his trousers well before she feels his smooth chest nestling into her shoulder blades, his bronze arms (covered in coarse blond hair) wrapping around hers, his heavy penis resting along the crease of her buttocks.

I love you, he whispers into her left ear. She smiles. I need you, he whispers into her right. She nods.

The unmistakable odour of maleness atomizing with the scents of stone and fern and rainwater. The vibration of as yet undisclosed childhood secrets in his chest. The trace of his fingertips along the vee of her hips. Ah, the probe of those fingertips! A silent and excruciating sign language telling folktales, amusing anecdotes, and childhood secrets until, finally, with a great shudder, a pair of scarlet macaws take flight from the underbrush, screaming.

Her bow skates across the bridge.

The two men wince.

She tries in vain to pick up where she left off.

Thank you, Stefan interrupts.

She blinks once, twice.

We'll be in touch, he says.

She stands. She exits.

Well? Eric asks, cocking his eyebrow.

Another pig, Stefan says, shaking his head. Don't you think?

Right, Eric says. Pig. Pig playing a pig with a pig.

Blackjack

WHEN YOU LET YOURSELF into the loft, you find Alex colouring in front of the television. Colouring is unfair. Alex is serious about becoming a visual artist in her spare time. Her art takes the dubious form of buying vintage copies of *Interview* magazine, choosing a black-and-white headshot of an 'eighties pop star, and transforming it into the image of someone else by reshading the eyes, cheeks, lips, and hair with a set of coloured pencils. So sad eyes of an awkward generation stare down at you from every turn, and your loft smells permanently of yesterday's news.

You spot the remains of a tuna sandwich on the coffee table. Judging by the hard white film ringing the milk glass next to it, Alex gave up on you a while ago. That she hasn't greeted you at the door is a bad sign. Normally, she stops whatever she's doing to give you a June Cleaver welcome-home kiss. You set your briefcase down and peer over her shoulder. She's busy turning Madonna—when she was young and beautiful—into jailhouse-rock-era Elvis. In a DA and sideburns, she's a dead ringer for K.D. Lang.

"Material Girl getting a makeover?" you say.

"Hardly her first," Alex says, choosing a violet pencil to accentuate Madonna's new five-o'clock shadow. You take heart. There's no trace of a fight brewing in Alex's voice. You place your hands on her shoulders and massage them. The muscles under your fingers neither tighten nor relax. If she had involuntarily tensed at your touch, you could have calculated how long it would take to coax her into bed.

And if she'd rolled her head up and smiled, you would have been in bed that much sooner. Your stomach flips over. Does her passivity mean she's getting used to your broken promises?

"I should have called," you say. "But Elaine snagged me into a meeting as I was on my way out the door."

Alex shrugs, letting your words thud unanswered to the carpet.

You want to shout, But it's true! I'm not lying! Because you actually did have to work late tonight. Elaine, your boss, really did insist you go over a few line items of next year's business plan. Unfortunately you've cried wolf about Elaine once too often.

You're cheating on Alex and she knows it.

Neither of you can decide what to do about it. Neither of you will bring it up. You both dread upsetting a decade of equilibrium. So both of you just live with this affair. It's the cold cadaver between you in bed at night. It's the real subject at dinner—whenever you drone on about the office, whenever she gossips about who's slipping it to whom at the department store. Hostility only surfaces in the form of complaints about wet towels on the bed after a shower or toilet seats left up.

"Guess you already ate," you say.

"I was hungry."

"I hope you didn't go to too much trouble fixing something."

"I'm smarter than that," she says, picking up a blood-red pencil, "I was going to stir fry. It's all chopped up and ready to go. But I set a time limit on you of seven o'clock. The veggies are still safe in the crisper."

"Any tuna left?" you ask.

"In the blue bowl next to the hummus."

"Do you hate me?" you ask, bending to wrap your arms around her neck.

"You ain't nothin' but a hound dog," she sings in a fair impersonation of The King.

"Don't be cruel," you singsong back.

"How about if I just pretend to be nice?" she says. "I'll fix you a sandwich. And then, in sullen gratitude, you'll take me out for an ice cream."

"I'd rather have two scoops of something else," you say, running your hands down the front of her t-shirt. Not true. That tuna sandwich sounds pretty good to you; you skipped lunch. And you can't immediately remember the last time you and Alex made love.

She moves your hands back to her shoulders. "Go take a shower," she says. "You'll feel better. And you stink."

"Okay," you say, wishing it didn't sound so much like an admission of guilt.

Michel is ten years younger than you, about the same age you were, actually, when you met Alex. He has no inkling of the complicated system of pulleys and levers that controls life. He doesn't even know yet that you're all marionettes. You've been seeing Michel on and off for over a month—lately more off than on. Trysts have been difficult to arrange. Alex is always home colouring after work, and fresh excuses for why you might need to pop out for a couple of hours have begun to verge on the absurd. It's been over a week now since you've spent time with Michel—apart from at the office. You have the fleeting urge to call him from your cell phone while Alex is having a pee in the bathroom after your shower. You suppress it.

Michel works in your IT department. You have always admired his looks but have not, until recently, registered him as anything other than that cute-French-boy-with-the-deeze-n-doze-accent-who-unfreezes-your-PC. Then, a month ago, you ran into him at a bar. Alex was in New York, at one of her rare trade shows. (By day, she's the buyer of fat-lady clothes for The Bay.) You had taken yourself out for a burger and beer—to a dive on Ste-Catherine you sometimes went to when you were single. After you ordered, you noticed Michel sitting alone in a booth, poring over a textbook. He didn't look up the entire time you ate. You skipped coffee and asked for the check, planning to slip out the side door. Then you thought: You're lonely, damn it. And you know him. Who cares if your job is several rungs above his on a corporate ladder? You paid up and went to his table.

Turns out, he was studying for an English test. He's enrolled in some ESL program at Concordia three nights a week. The two of you chatted about the office for five minutes (boring); then about where each of you is from (he, a farm near Sherbrooke; you, Laval); then about which neighbourhoods you now live in (you, a loft in Old Montreal—no mention of Alex; he, a studio in the Village); then about where you both usually hang out (you, no place special—no mention of Alex; he, at that bar.)

Things loosened up when you started drilling him on his irregular tenses. With a purpose, you felt some of your charm returning. It delighted you to find out how much you knew instinctively about English. You liked playing teacher. When did you realize you were trying to pick him up? Probably after he complained that Anglos usually treat him like a child. He said they're never patient enough to let him express himself. You felt a strong desire to show him you were different. You ordered more beer.

Around midnight, you asked him if he wanted to go out dancing. He yawned and told you he'd rather go back to his apartment and make out. Language barrier or direct nature?

Sure, you said.

His place was very small: a kitchenette, a tiny bathroom, another small room dominated by a bed. An enormous framed illustration of *La Civilisation Perdue de l'Atlantide*. It excited you that there was no room to be conventionally social. Michel made some herbal tea and you both sipped it out of bowls, sitting cross-legged on his bed. He slurped noisily (lustfully, you thought) then reached over to the night stand and grabbed a deck of cards.

"Do you play?" he asked, shuffling.

"I know a few games," you said.

"Teach me," he said, handing you the deck. You froze. Put on the spot, your authority evaporated. Those countless games of hearts that you'd played with your sister and grandmother suddenly felt like someone else's life. You were mesmerized by shocking blue eyes, skin that ought to be illegal.

"I don't remember the rules to anything," you stammered.

Disdain materialized at the corners of Michel's mouth. Taking the deck back, he lit an Export A and took several drags. "All right," he exhaled. "We will play the Blackjack. You know how?"

You nodded.

"No wild card, eh? Each game will cost ten dollar. First I deal, then you. If we tie, we continue to thirty-one."

"Ten bucks?" you said, trying to keep the anxiety out of your voice. "Isn't that a little steep?"

Michel looked up from his dealing. "You could maybe win a lot of money," he said.

"Or lose a lot," you said.

He shrugged and started to collect the cards back.

"How about a dollar a game?"

"That is not so interesting."

"But I only have about fifteen dollars in my wallet," you said.

"You can write a cheque," he smiled.

You panicked. What if you were to lose a hundred dollars? Alex usually scrutinized every line of the monthly bank statement. She caught a surprising number of errors that way.

"So deal," you said.

You played intently for two hours. Michel offered you a hit of ecstasy and, though you had never even smoked pot before, you swallowed it. At two o'clock, you were very high and ahead sixty dollars. Michel declared he'd had enough and reached for his cheque book. You told him he didn't have to—after all, it was just a game.

"I would have gladly taken your money," he said.

And then he began to unbutton your shirt.

Alex's favourite ice cream place is over in the Village. It's a hell of walk from the loft but, because it's all-natural organic blah-blah-blah, it's the only one she'll patronize. She's into all that at the moment. Herbalism. Yoga. Acupuncture.

You amble your way through Chinatown in companionable silence. You hardly ever walk side by side anymore. One or the other of you is always lagging behind to peer into a shop window or banter hello to an acquaintance in the neighbourhood.

Near the Berri metro stop, you're startled by a man who looks exactly like your father. But it can't be him; he died last spring. This imposter turns out to be your own reflection in the window of an ATM kiosk. These unplanned encounters with yourself irritate you.

You've gotten very careful about mirrors. You used to shave before showering in the morning. Now you've reversed the process. Now you make yourself squint through the steam and condensation build-up. You're already on your walk to work by the time the fog lifts.

"Do you think I look like my father?" you ask Alex.

"Spit and image. Why?"

"But he looked so paternal, like Ward Cleaver."

"Ward Cleaver made my nipples hard," Alex says.

"I've aged," you sigh. You know this is a complete *non sequitur*.

"Thank God," she says.

Alex is no help at times like these. What times?—be specific. Times when you get mired in the funhouse mirrors of your current identity.

Alex has always been a better judge of character than you. She knows which acquaintances will turn out to be friends, which of your colleagues will eventually try to stab you in the back. She hasn't read a book in years, though. And she's perfectly happy to buy The Bay's fat-lady clothes for a living. It was you who went to the good schools. It's you who has the high-powered executive job, you who makes the big money. Yet Alex finishes every Sunday crossword you abandon.

"Why are you smiling?" she asks now.

"I love you," you say. And you mean it. You don't tell her this very often—not once in the last three years, in fact. Because you've both categorized I-love-you as one of those overly explicit clichés.

"You're a freak," Alex says in the same tone of voice as I-love-you-too.

"Fuck you," you say.

"Why waste wishes on what you can have?" she says.

Ten years ago, your sister, Patricia, introduced you to Alex at a party. You were both sharing an apartment your dad paid for in St. Laurent while you got your careers off the ground. Patricia and Alex were sales clerks together at the downtown Eatons. It was sort of a set-up and, true to Patricia's predictions, you liked Alex immediately. When you asked her which training program she was in, she admitted up-front that she slapped makeup on old ladies' faces for eight hours a day. She wanted a Molson's when you offered to fetch her a drink.

She wasn't any more chatty than she is now. About all she wanted to know from you at that party was whether you played piano as well as Patricia claimed. When you said yes, she told you to prove it on the concert grand in the front room. You played for twenty minutes— anything that came to your head. You even made things up. Alex sat on the bench beside you, sipping her beer. Whenever you stopped, she said "more," and you played more. Finally, when your fingers began to cramp, you turned to her and said, "That's it." She protested and you insisted, "No, I'm finished. Why don't you play something for me. Do you know how?" Alex played a nocturne by Chopin. She played it beautifully; better than you would have.

The two of you stuck together for the rest of the evening. Patricia, on the other hand, left the party early. She'd met a salesman who insisted on taking her to see the sunrise from his warehouse on the waterfront. At about two in the morning, you asked Alex if she was ready to leave. She was welcome to crash at your apartment around the corner; God only knew when Patricia would be getting back. Alex declined. Was she sure? The two of you could go to her place instead. No thanks. How about a movie sometime.

Ten years later, neither of you can remember which CDs originally belonged to whom. Mathematically, you've eaten every single dish Alex knows how to cook—at least five hundred times. She knows every one of your family stories by heart. She helped your mother make all the arrangements for your father's funeral. Not only have you begun to sound alike—you've picked up most of each other's verbal idiosyncrasies—but you're beginning to look alike, somehow. Tired.

You have never asked Alex to marry you. She has never questioned why.

At the ice cream parlour, you buy cones and join the small crowd loitering around the front steps to watch the sun set. No one wants to be inside tonight. It's one of those rare end-of-summer beauties, the kind that never happen on weekends.

"Last year at this time we rented that cottage on Lake Champlain,"

Alex says, "Remember how beautiful the sunsets were?"

You nod.

"We were practically naked, day and night."

"Where did you rent?" asks the man sitting next to Alex on the top step. "I'll have to get the place next door." He's ridiculously handsome, wearing a suit.

Alex laughs and—typical Alex—begins to explain your complicated friend-of-a-friend connection on Isle LaMotte. Meanwhile, you see another startling face in your peripheral vision—someone who looks exactly like Michel. But it's no imposter this time. Michel is strolling down the block, with a tall blond man your age. They're coming to this very shop for an ice cream. At first you look down, to quell the icy panic of a whole scoop of all-natural Heavenly Hash lodged in your throat. Then you decide to look directly at him as he approaches the bottom step—brave it out. Why hasn't he noticed you yet? He's deep in conversation with blondie. You think: they walk just like they're a couple. "Hey!" you say—too brightly—your arms buzzing and tingling with the danger of the moment.

"Oh hello," Michel says. "It's a beautiful night, no?"

"Yes," you say.

"You are well?" he asks.

"Fine," you say.

"This is Eric," he says, presenting blondie as an afterthought. You introduce yourself and then Alex to Michel and Eric. A very long moment elapses.

"Well, we go now to eat an ice cream," Michel says, pointing inside the shop.

"See you later," you say. "Nice meeting you, Eric." So that's why Michel hasn't called in so long. Feelings of jealousy are hardly appropriate.

As soon as they're inside, Alex turns to you and says, "How do you know someone that cute?" The guy in the suit laughs, and Alex joins in. You feel oddly stung. Why does this seem implausible enough to joke about with a complete stranger?

"He's just one of the computer geeks at my company," you say.

"I'm in the market for a new laptop," Alex says.

"Cute," you say to their fresh outbreak of laughter.

Just keep laughing. It'll prevent you from pressing your nose against the plate glass window to chronicle Michel's every move. Because you can see things so clearly, so differently, in your mind: Michel asleep next to you, his curled hand across your chest. His fingers forming a fragile shell; the concealed palm glowing in the first light of day. Alex is still in New York, you are still in ecstasy in Michel's bed, sixty dollars richer. You insert, so very gently, your finger into that hand on your chest, the act triggering an instinctual response from him—he squeezes it in his sleep. Now you see the moment in a different light: you are plugged into him. His sexual current makes your fingers hum, then your hand, then your arm. The blinds create a grid of sunlight on his face. His eyelids glow pink in one of these bars of light. He slowly opens them and his pupils glitter like Madonna's.

"Let's go," you say to Alex. Then for the guy in the suit's benefit: "I've got to be at the office early for an important conference call."

It's Alex who breaks the silence during your Pinocchio stumble back to the loft. "Sorry about being so bitchy when you got home. I understand about your job—I really do. I just don't feel like being understanding sometimes."

"I know," you say.

Alex is in a good mood, now. She really loves walks and chatting with random strangers and ice cream. You've made up for the lost dinner. You can tell by the way she's moving that she'll want to make love when you get home.

What do you want?

You want to make a detour of about twenty-five years to someplace quiet and young—to your father's lap or a tree fort or an empty refrigerator box. At the very least, you would like to slink off to one of the bars you used to haunt when you were single to get good and drunk. Where could you go where it would never be necessary to think about the things you do and why you do them? Some vast mythological city—Atlantis—with the power to swallow you whole, make you to disappear. Or London, maybe. You've never been to London.

But you can't disappear right now. Because if you withdraw from Alex, if you shut down on her right now, she'll figure it all out. You have very little choice, the way you see it. You have to screw her when you get home.

Dan, in re: Christine

1. WEEKEND IN HELL

The point, of course, is to plot your own murder. But Dan is happy to defer to Christine's opinion regarding his. To Christine, suffocation seems appropriate. She is against anything overly violent; none of them knows Dan all that well. Everyone agrees with her about this, though it is unanimously decided Dan should be among the first to go. He hasn't brought a costume.

His death opens with a wide-angle shot of Friday's masquerade party in full swing. The camera pans the living room in medium close-up: from a sultan and Cleopatra doing The Pony on a coffee table to Salvador Dalí mixing a gin and tonic for a man dressed like Barbie. It follows the progression of a lit joint down the sofa from Miss America to Hillary Clinton to Elmer Fudd. Suddenly Elmer Fudd (Christine) asks if anyone has seen Dan. A mad search ensues until Miss America lifts one of the sofa cushions and exposes his upper body shaking with laughter, a rubber duck stuffed in his mouth. Christine exclaims, This isn't a quiet fall getaway in Vermont! The rest chime in, It's a weekend in hell!

That's it, really. The rubber duck is removed from his mouth. Someone hands him a Labatts. Dan is dead for the rest of the weekend.

In a way it is a relief, to have the focus of attention shift away from him—the new guy, Christine's date. The problem is, she too seems to lose all interest. As soon as the party gets rolling again, she disappears outside with a sad clown. Upon her return, she takes Cleopatra's place on the coffee table. Dan later finds her embroiled in a heated game of Mille Bornes. He can't help it; he begins to get annoyed. He has just been suffocated, after all. He's feeling a little vulnerable. He decides it must be some kind of test: the sink-or-swim method of social acceptance. Trying to remain calm, he goes to the kitchen to get himself another beer. The camera crew is setting up near the microwave. A woman named Ann is planning to be cooked alive. She wasn't warned to bring a costume either.

Cut to an extreme close-up of a pair of gloved hands. They stalk Ann as she reheats a bowl of chili. The hands grab her around the neck, force her head into the microwave. She rasps for help, but to no avail. After a moment, she stops struggling. Cut to Barbie reaching into the refrigerator for a beer. The microwave's timer goes off, mysteriously. Barbie opens the door to peek inside. Cut to an extreme close-up of a jack-o'-lantern which has been nuked beyond recognition, Ann's glasses perched on its deflated features. Then a wide-angle shot of Barbie screaming, My God, that's no pumpkin; it's Ann McLeod! before falling to the floor in a dead faint. Dissolve.

Dan applauds with the rest as they take their bows. But when a cold hand grips the back of his neck, he jumps about a foot. "Glad to see you're fitting in," whispers Christine into his ear. "Most people find us a little ferocious at first." She yawns theatrically. "I'm ready for bed. How about you?" Dan nods, not so sure. She wraps her arm around his waist and leads him to one of the bedrooms. Is it his imagination, or do her friends nod knowingly? He asks her if she's won her card game. "Of course," she says.

He soon discovers she is a virgin. They are making love in one of the bunk beds. "You can tell?" she asks, dismayed. "Rats. I thought that was just grope novel mythology. Do you mind, Dan? I know I'm a bit overdue at twenty-three. But I am Catholic." He tells her he doesn't mind at all; that, to the contrary, he's honoured. She laughs and warns him to reserve his judgment until after. He proceeds with caution. As he nears climax, he asks if he's hurting her. She laughs again, which makes him lose his erection. Apologizing, she explains how difficult it is to take seriously, losing her virginity to a corpse.

***

He is the first person up on Saturday morning, except for Claude who has not bothered to go to bed. Claude is smoking on the sofa and leafing through a faded *Ladies' Home Journal*. He is still dressed as Salvador Dalí, though the curls of his eyebrow-pencil mustache have smeared. Dan says good morning. Claude says, "Bonjour, I thought you were dead." They both laugh hollowly as Claude makes room on the sofa. He's already mixed a pitcher of Bloody Marys. As he pours Dan one, he tells him how glad he is that Christine has finally found a nice boy. Dan can't help but mention his obvious competition in that department—because he wonders, not for the first time, what he's doing there.

When Christine called mid-week to invite him to her family's cabin in Vermont, he said sure, he'd love to go, without hesitating. Christine of awkward friend-of-a-friend party conversation in Old Montreal, Christine of two mezzo-mezzo dates at the film archive on St-Denis, Christine of recent dirty dreams. She advised him to get out of work early on Friday, be packed and waiting on his porch for her by three. He would have agreed to anything. It never occurred to him that she might swing into his driveway a full hour late with three handsome men grinning from the back seat. He'd already filled in all the blanks with long walks in the woods, intimate dinners at rustic inns, brandy and love-making in front of a roaring fire. Had she really forgotten to mention how this particular weekend was an annual tradition among a dozen or so of her artist friends? Well, yes, she had. Should he brace himself for any other little surprises? No, definitely not, except for the costume party. And the video project.

Regarding his romantic competition, Claude now assures Dan with a flourish of celery stalk that all the boys are gay—except maybe for the married one. In the course of their chat, Claude confesses he is the least talented dancer with Les Grands Ballets Canadiens—this without a trace of false modesty. Dan likes that. They decide to make breakfast for the rest.

Christine cannot be gotten out of bed. She claims to have drunk far too much during the party, has given herself the hangover to end all hangovers. When Dan tells her breakfast is ready, she races to the toilet and throws up. All attempts to reassure her that the night before was really special for him are absorbed by her misery. He heads for the kitchen to eat. She continues to vomit for most of the morning.

As soon as the breakfast dishes are out of the way, the gloved assailant wreaks more havoc. Mary Margaret is liberally covered with ketchup and stabbed in the shower (an obligatory nod to *Psycho*). Joanne is strangled in bed with the belt of her bathrobe. Claude is thrown off the sun porch to the slate patio below. Since Dan is already dead, he does most of the camera work. He films each corpse being dragged to a growing pile near the fireplace.

By lunch, Christine is feeling better. They all decide to spend the afternoon outlet shopping. As they wind their way down into town, they ooh and ahh dutifully at peak foliage and the occasional covered bridge. In a scenic lull, Dan asks Christine how she will be handling her own death. She smiles for the first time that day, shrugs. She hasn't decided. The married couple next to them announce they will be slain together.

Fade in on a long shot of the Ralph Lauren parking lot. Christine strolls up to the trunk of Mary Margaret's Cutlass, carrying two shopping bags. She hums as she opens the back with a key. The camera lens zooms in on her as she gasps in horror, dropping her bags to the pavement. Cut to a close-up of the trunk's interior. The married couple are lying in each other's arms, lips locked in a fatal kiss, bodies bound in a set of hunter-orange jumper cables.

When Dan yells "Cut!" everyone agrees this is the best one yet. Christine excuses herself and runs into the store. She gets sick twice more that afternoon; once in J. Crew's bathroom, once at the side of the road during the drive back to the cabin. She apologizes to everyone, swearing she'll never drink again, insisting she isn't feeling quite herself. Claude comments that it must be love.

Dan suggests she take it easy for the rest of the day. She invites him to lie with her on the sofa. They fool around a little under a quilt, do several crossword puzzles out of yellowed Sunday papers. Her friends ignore them. Some are busy planning an elaborate, multiple hanging to take place at sunrise. Some are playing a take-no-prisoners game of Monopoly by the fire. Others prepare dinner and ferry drinks around the room. Christine whispers to Dan that the sofa is an island. He nods. They watch together as her friends swirl and eddy by. He tells Christine about growing up in Toronto. She tells him about growing up in Sherbrooke. He reveals his ambition to become an international marketing guru and travel the world by the time he's thirty. She tells him her future as a biomedical engineer is, as yet, unclear. When he gets up to go to the bathroom, she urges him to hurry back.

Upon his return, however, he finds Claude in Christine's arms. He hangs back to eavesdrop. She is telling him she just isn't sure. She is worried about how earnest he is all the time, about how little he makes her laugh. Claude says, "Honey, forget about his sense of humour; he's gorgeous. You want laughs, you give us a call." At this, they burst into a fit of giggles. Dan wanders into the kitchen, offering to chop something up for dinner.

Just before they sit down to eat, they decide to watch what they've videotaped so far. The deaths are hilarious, in part due to the amateurish way they are filmed, in part to how rapidly one transpires after another. They are all gasping for breath and wiping their eyes—all except Christine. It seems a whole lot less funny to Dan, watching her watch the video. She is staring at the screen so intently, picking at her fingernails with her teeth. "There's something not quite right," she keeps whispering to herself.

Their sex is ... interesting ... that night. What Christine doesn't know about technique, she makes up for in determination. Catholic or not, she is fairly uninhibited about her body. She hasn't yet gotten to that point where she considers herself a sacred temple of hushed and hallowed halls, an altar reserved for respectful worship. Christine tells him she sees them both as exquisite mechanical devices, as gold watches that need to be dismantled in order to discover what makes them tick. Dan thinks: it must be the engineer in her. She tells him the word for orgasm in French means "little death," which, now that she's had one, seems entirely apt. What would be the point, she asks, unless they were both driving toward some sort of shared oblivion? Dan thinks she talks too much in the sack.

As soon as he dozes off, she gets up and goes to the bathroom.

When she crawls back to bed, sweaty and smelling of peppermint toothpaste, he tells her she can't possibly have a hangover; that it must be some weird strain of stomach flu.

"It isn't the flu, Dan," she says, stroking his chest. "It's the chemo. I had a treatment on Thursday afternoon. Don't worry. It's got to be almost out of me by now."

She explains how there are four different chemo treatments for leukemia, that she's just started number three. The last one did little more than strengthen her fingernails. This one will make her lose her hair. This one won't work either. But she's doing it for her parents, though she herself would prefer not to die bald.

"So now you know," she sighs. "You're fucking a corpse, too. At least I won't be checking out a cue ball and a virgin." Dan tells her he is very sorry—which sounds stupid, even to him. So he adds that he feels honoured to be holding her v-card.

"I used you," she says, flatly.

"Chose me," he corrects. "You chose me." They make love again. And then she makes him promise not to tell the others. She's certain they all suspect the worst. But she prefers things the way they are, with no one bringing it up. Dan finds the whole charade a little odd. Remember, she says, they're mostly all Catholic.

At breakfast, Christine declares she's figured out what the movie is missing: a murderer. It won't make any sense otherwise. She offers, since she is one of the remaining few alive after the hangings, to fill the necessary role. Everyone thinks this appropriate. (More knowing glances?) After all, the video was her idea. And it is her family's cabin.

In the final scene, a pile of dead bodies zooms into focus. The camera pans around to Christine who sits on the sofa staring at the corpses, gloved and silent. It follows her to the kitchen where she closes the microwave door, wipes a knife clean before returning it to a drawer, coils a length of rope and stores it under the sink. Cut to the master bedroom where she rethreads a terry cord through the loops of a bathrobe lying on a chair. The camera then follows her as she makes her way to the front door, slinging a set of orange jumper cables over her shoulder. En route, she flicks off light switches, lowers the thermostat, retrieves her coat from the hall closet. Zoom in for a close-up of her face: she is smiling an odd sort of smile. She whispers: This is not a quiet fall getaway in Vermont. It's a weekend in hell. She turns and closes the door behind her. Dissolve.

2. MARRIAGE PANIC

Pink phone messages now fill Dan with terror. Before Christine, he used to let them stack up in his mail slot, a fluffy pink nest. He used to sweep them all into Margie-the-Receptionist's wastebasket every Friday afternoon without looking at them. He used to believe the onus was on the message-leaver to call back. Before Christine, that is.

Call Christine NOW. URGENT. It's Tuesday afternoon. Dan is just getting in from lunch. "Who's this Christine?" Margie asks. She is frankly meddlesome when it comes to the personal lives of her superiors. Dan dislikes her for her faint mustache. "All of a sudden I'm getting twenty calls a day from this Christine person. Is she a client of ours? She made it sound like a matter of life and death."

Dan closes his office door on her question.

Of course Christine is away from her desk when he tries to reach her. And though he tells himself over and over that that's just the way she is, urgent, of course he frets for the rest of the afternoon, calling back every hour or so. Each time, Christine's receptionist tells him she's so sorry but he's just missed her; when she's in the lab she's not to be disturbed. Christine harvests proteins of interest for a drug company that confects miraculous cures: blood clotting agents for hemophiliacs, missing rungs in the DNA ladders of autistic children, sera for people with AIDS. She's entry-level, though, so she works on the company's more cosmetic concerns—new acne creams and wrinkle removers, that sort of thing. The receptionist assures Dan that Christine has been given every one of his messages.

When his phone finally rings, it is after ten. He is at home and has fallen asleep on the sofa with the TV on, the phone resting on his chest.

"Dan!" Christine says, slightly out of breath. "I'm glad I finally caught you."

"What's wrong?" he croaks, not entirely sure where he is.

"What are you doing on Saturday night?"

"Saturday?"

"Good. Listen. There's the annual swing ball at the Queen Elizabeth Hotel. I need a date. I've taken the liberty of reserving a tux for you—you don't own one do you?"

"Wait a minute, wait a minute." Dan wants to say, What if I don't happen to be free on Saturday? But he knows Christine knows that's unlikely. "I don't know how to swing dance," he says.

"Neither do I. That's why I've enrolled us in a crash course at Arthur Murray. The one over on René Lévesque. Three lessons; Wednesday, Thursday and Friday from seven to nine."

"You mean you've never been to one of these swing balls?"

"Along with the swing lessons, you get one waltz and one foxtrot. I got a deal from Arthur Murray because I said it was for our wedding. Thirty per cent off. It's called the Marriage Panic course—isn't that cute?"

By now Dan's head has cleared enough for him to realize there is no emergency. She is in no danger, needs no immediate medical attention. "Christine," he says—a sigh, really— "you have chemo on Thursday."

"Okay. So we go to two out of three and fake the rest."

"Might I remind you that by Friday you are rarely up to trotting."

"Dan!"

He does not give in when she offers to skip chemo this week in order to make all the lessons. He does not give in when she accuses him of no longer being the spontaneous corpse she fell in like with. He gives in when she swears she'll take Claude instead. Claude dances with Les Grands Ballets Canadiens.

"This is really that important to you?"

"I never ask you for anything." Wildly untrue; they both know it.

"I have to wear a tux?"

"You're the greatest, Fred. I'll meet you in the lobby of Arthur Murray at a quarter to seven. Bring soft-soled shoes. Smooch."

It takes Dan a full ten minutes to get the joke. Fred. Fred Astaire.

Their instructor's name is Roger. He kind of looks like Fred Astaire; or maybe he's just trying to: his socks are the same colour yellow as his cardigan. The three of them are standing in the middle of the parquet floor, an island of calm. Couples in their forties swirl around the perimeter, dipping and swooping to an Anne Murray song. All the men look gay and are wearing bowling shoes. All the women wear Princess Margaret hair styles and have plucked their eyebrows away.

Roger is telling them he's a real hard ass. He runs his Marriage Panic course like boot camp. Over the next three nights, he will change their lives forever. They'll hate him, he predicts, but respect him. Not only will Christine and Dan soon be husband and wife, they will become partners in the dance of life. Dan focuses his attention on the mirrored ball above Roger's head to keep from howling. Boot camp! How seriously can he take a man lecturing to them in a purple rayon shirt, knotted at the bellybutton like Carmen Miranda? Christine jabs Dan in the side with her elbow. But enough chit-chat, Roger says, let's get right down to business. Foxtrot. Backs straight, shoulders squared.

Foxtrot. A ballroom dance in duple time that alternates slow walking steps with quick running steps. The object is to draw imaginary rectangles with your feet.

Dan is hopeless. He cannot hear the beat of the music. He could have told them both. He has never been able to hear music. He worked his way through half the instruments in the school band before his parents finally bought him a pony.

No one can call Dan a quitter, though. He makes the best of it. A promise is a promise. He thinks of Christine every Thursday: sitting in that dimly lit hospital room, reading last year's magazines while a plastic bag of poisonous chemicals drips into her body. She does it for her parents, a gift. As long as she keeps going to chemo, they can believe there's hope. In the meantime, she makes the best of it. She has become great friends with three other Thursday afternoon patients. They call themselves Death Row, have had t-shirts made up. They watch the afternoon talk shows, pick on each other, play mean-spirited bridge. For April Fool's, Christine smuggled red food colouring into the ward. She dyed the only guy's treatment bag while he napped, then woke him up screaming "Oh my God, there's something wrong, your transfusion's going in reverse, get a nurse!" April Fool. The trick, according to Christine, is to find the humour in every situation. Dan is not known for his sense of humour.

He now straightens his back, squares his shoulders. But he crashes repeatedly into her, stepping all over her toes. She smiles encouragement, squeezes his arm. There are tears in her eyes. After several minutes, Roger takes pity on them. They only have two more classes together, he warns. Desperate times call for desperate measures. Roger swaps places with Christine to show them how a woman can lead without looking like she's doing it. It works. Dan seems able keep up with the tempo as long as he follows. Humiliated doesn't begin to describe how he feels, gliding across the room to Kenny Rogers in the arms of Roger-the-dance-instructor. And the worst of it: seeing himself reflected to infinity in the floor-to-ceiling mirrors, appearing to be in complete control.

Dan is beginning to lose control of the work situation. After lunch on Thursday, there is a memo on his desk from Margie-the-Receptionist. To: Dan. In Re: Christine. Cc: virtually everyone on the planet. May I remind you I am not your personal secretary nor am I your events coordinator. My duties include taking those messages which pertain to your business interests. They do not include being verbally mistreated by your love interests. I am happy to discuss this with you as soon as you are freed up from more pressing duties.

"What's this about, Margie?"

"Your personal life is intruding on your job performance, Dan. A little friendly advice. Watch your ass."

"Oh come off it. You're on the phone half the day with your girlfriends. Christine doesn't call that often."

"She called me a bitch this morning."

"When did she call? Where was I?"

"Who the hell knows where you are half the time."

Dan knows she's right; he had better watch his ass. He is sitting at his desk waiting for his boss to summon him for an explanation of Margie's memo. His work has been slipping. Two of his reports have recently been returned with "dig deeper" Post-it notes on them. He has begun to lose sight of why he should spend nine, ten, sometimes twelve hours a day at this place. Christine. Maybe he should just tell his boss the truth: that it's impossible for him to imagine how this job fits into his future plans; that lately, it's impossible for him to imagine the future, full stop.

The phone rings. It is not his boss. It's Christine. "Where have you been?" she sobs. "They canned me when I got into the lab this morning. They're calling it a leave of absence."

"Oh God. Why?"

"Christ Dan, I disappear every Thursday afternoon, puke all day Friday. I'm either pregnant or dying, neither of which is very career-minded."

"They have no right."

"Sure they do. I'm months behind on that cure for baldness."

"Where are you now?"

"At home."

"I'll be right over."

"Don't be absurd. It's all spilt milk. I just need to vent. I'll see you at Arthur Murray."

"But you have chemo."

"I told you, I'm skipping it. I'm going to that ball, Dan."

The next phone call is his boss. Dan has visions of closing the door to his office and waltzing out of the firm for good, without ever turning back. Except perhaps to tell Margie over his shoulder that she is a bitch. But he doesn't. He heads for his boss' office, avoiding Margie's satisfied receptionist smirk. He needs this fucking job. Tuxedoes don't grow on trees.

Waltz. A ballroom dance in three-four time with a strong accent on the first beat and a basic foot pattern of step-step-close.

Roger says: if they plan to get anything right, it had better be the waltz. Will Christine be wearing white? She smiles. Yes, she says, big and white and puffy, with petticoats. And what will Dan be wearing? A morning coat, Christine whispers, a cut-away; they haven't decided yet about the spats. Wonderful, says Roger. But if they're going to look like Scarlett and Rhett, hadn't they better be able to do the charity ball scene? Do they really want to lurch through their first dance together as husband and wife?

They both shake their heads no.

"What are we going to do?" Dan whispers. They are lurching around Arthur Murray while Roger claps out the tempo. They should be spinning on the first beat. Roger says two rotations a second is optimal Viennese.

"We're going to keep it small," Christine grins. "Under a hundred people. My parents belong to this really beautiful country club in Sherbrooke. It has these gorgeous French doors that open out onto a terrace overlooking the golf course."

"Will you be serious? We're in deep shit here."

"No," she says, laying her head on his chest. "I will not be serious. Do you hear me, Dan? I will not be serious. I think lilies. Callas, everywhere. And why the hell not? Spats for you. Spats for all the ushers. Silk stockings for all the bridesmaids."

One moment she's debating the virtues of sit-down dinner versus buffet-style with Roger, the next she's wiping away tears as she whispers one-two-three, one-two-three, watch the toes, Dan. It's all getting to be a bit much for him. Christine's ex-lab group thinks it has found a cure for male pattern baldness. It seems to work on rats. Time to test it on humans. Excusing himself, Dan races to the men's room. He dry-heaves to the strains of Strauss.

On Friday, Dan brings Margie a small bouquet of flowers. The little card apologizes for any misunderstanding. She is cool to him, but impressed. She offers to get him coffee, since she's already on her way over to the machine. Later, he asks her if she needs anything from the sandwich shop around the corner. He surprises himself by having a very productive day; he is able to get through a fair amount of the work teetering in piles on his desk.

Mid-afternoon, Margie transfers a call from Christine without comment. Christine seems depressed but insists everything's fine.

She says she's enjoying unemployment. She's been able to clean—really clean—her apartment for the first time in months. And it amazes her how easily she is able to follow the plotlines of the morning soaps she used to watch in college. Finally she comes out with what's bothering her: every single member of Death Row has called her wondering why she didn't show up for this week's treatment. They were all worried she was dead. Dan tells her not to be late for Arthur Murray. They will need every moment of instruction they've paid for. He writes out a Post-it note to himself to swing by the tux place after work. He plans to show Christine the time of her life.

Swing. A jazz dance in moderate tempo with a lilting syncopation. Characterized by the triple step: side-together-side, side-together-side, rock step.

When he gets to Arthur Murray, Christine and Roger are already fox-trotting. Though she is smiling, putting up a brave front, she looks like hell. Her face is pale gray and covered with a sheen of perspiration, so maybe she went to chemo after all. She's obviously not able to concentrate on what she's doing. Dan wonders how she will ever be able to make it through dinner and cocktails tomorrow night, an evening of dancing. He wonders why she would put herself through such an ordeal. When Christine sees him, he waves. She waves back, blows him a kiss. His heart! His poor, weak heart.

The swing lesson is exhausting for both of them. Christine is having difficulty with all the hopping around. She is drenched and her breath comes in short, hard gasps. Roger shakes his head and tells them they look like a couple of monkeys dropped on hot coals. They decide to take a break after about twenty minutes. Roger ducks into the employee lounge to make a phone call, Dan walks Christine over to the water cooler.

"Conditioned response," she assures him. "It's Friday, and my stomach thinks it should be puking." She sighs. "There's no frigging way we're going to learn how to swing dance tonight. Panic is right."

"We've got another hour."

"Oh please, Dan! Even if your two left feet manage some sort of epiphany, I won't be able to keep up. My heart's getting too weak."

"We're not so bad at the other two."

"Well, Dan, we're not going to a foxtrot ball, are we?"

Dan takes her into his arms and encourages her to cry it all out. When Roger comes over, he suggests they get back on the horse that threw them. Christine's face is still buried in Dan's neck. Dan asks if they could please have a little waltz. Roger strongly urges they first work out a pared-down swing routine. Dan reminds him how important their first dance as husband and wife will be. Roger acquiesces and puts on the Strauss record.

Christine is too much of a mess to lead. She keeps whispering, I can't, I can't, I just want to go home. So Dan leads—badly at first. But he gets better, especially when Christine wipes her nose with the back of her hand and begins to count one-two-three, one-two-three. And eventually, mercifully, the room blurs. Because they're finally spinning on the first beat, spinning and spinning, shooting for two rotations a second.

3. FUCKING BLIND

Dan directs Christine's head a little closer to the plastic dish tub in his lap. He doesn't want her to get puke all over the bedspread. It is the eve of Christine's twenty-fourth birthday—moments, actually, before midnight. They have not been out clubbing in the Village with Mary Margaret and Joanne and the gay boys. There were no lavishly wrapped gifts waiting for her when she got home from the clinic, no bottles of champagne chilling in the freezer compartment, no engagement ring under her pillow. Dan pulls her chestnut curls out of the way, holding them in a ponytail at the nape of her neck. He hopes they won't break off in his hand, her curls. The chemo. No surprise party. Tonight's only surprise: that Christine will make it to twenty-four.

"I'm drowning," she gasps.

"Sorry," Dan says, tugging on the ponytail to raise her head out of the tub. "Finished?"

"I don't know how much more I can take of this," she tells him.

He wonders about this himself. He hands her a tissue from the night stand—to wipe her mouth. "Oh look," he says noticing the digital alarm clock, "it's your birthday." She doesn't comment. Keep it light. He begins to sing "Happy Birthday" in a Donald Duck voice, coaxing Christine to lie back. She manages a weak giggle. He tells her to rest a bit before getting up to brush her teeth. Then he climbs out of bed with the tub, asking her if she needs anything from the bathroom—a glass of water, an aspirin?

"A gun," she sighs.

Just keep it light. About all he can afford, he says, is the bullets. He takes the tub to the toilet, dumps it out, flushes. It's periwinkle blue, the tub. He rinses it under the shower before drying it with one of the rags under the sink. Christine is asleep when he returns to the bedroom. He sets the tub down on the floor, on her side of the bed. She lies there motionless, as usual, making no sound. You'd need to hold a mirror under her nose to be sure. He knows this will soon change. At least the neighbours have stopped calling the police when the screaming starts. He climbs into bed beside her. She jumps. "What?" she says. She is still asleep.

"Nothing. Happy birthday." Whispering to no one.

—Your chart is a map of the sky at the moment of your birth. It records where each of the planets are as they travel though the Zodiac. If the Zodiac is the whole universe, this circle, each slice of the pie represents a different house.

—So I'm in the house of Leo.

—Actually, no. You're here, on earth, at the very center of the chart. The sun is in Leo, so Leo is your sun sign. The planet coming up over the eastern horizon—your rising sign—is Capricorn. Curious. The ruling planet for Capricorn is Saturn which comes up over the horizon in the very same hour. But Saturn's in a different house, at twenty degrees Aquarius. Very intriguing, this whole configuration.

—I bet you say that to everyone.

—Saturn in Aquarius is quite unusual. It indicates uniqueness, eccentricity; a lover of freedom and independence, the dance of life. But the way it's aspected in your chart looks like you're living life in reverse.

—In reverse?

—Like you're born old and get younger with each passing year.

—So that means I'm going to look fabulous at fifty, right?

—Not exactly.

—How not exactly?

—The younger we are, the more dependent we are on others.

Last Friday afternoon, Christine went to an astrologer with Claude. It was his early birthday present to her. At first, Christine refused flat-out to go. She had no interest in the tearoom where several members of Les Grands Ballets regularly had their fortunes told. But Claude wouldn't take no for an answer. (Dan likes Claude a lot. He is the only member of Christine's crowd who knows for certain about her leukemia. He's HIV-positive.) There's an astrologer at this tearoom, Claude said, who is guaranteed to be wrong about everything—who never fails to miss by a mile. Finally Christine agreed to go, as long as whoever read her chart couldn't see into the future. She was elated when she called Dan after the reading: she would live forever, make loads and loads of money, get married, have three children, live happily ever after. Dan wondered how he could possibly top this as a birthday present.

Later that evening, Christine sprained her ankle. She fainted on her way to the bathroom. Dan was not there; he'd decided to sleep at his own apartment that night. When she came to, she was lying in the hallway with her right foot twisted beneath her. To get to the phone, she'd had to drag herself into the kitchen. He will never forget the way he found her: sitting on the stool near the window, staring down into the alley behind her building. She was crying. There was a trail of dried puke as wide as her body across the linoleum. She wouldn't look at him while he examined her, wouldn't look at him while he called a cab to take her to the emergency room. Her ankle had begun to turn the colour of week-old bananas. He decided to move in.

—Does longevity run in your family?

—I don't know; I'm adopted.

—Well it looks like you're going to be around for a while.

—What makes you say that?

—Nothing much in the house that rules health. Doesn't appear to be one of the issues you have to deal with in this life.

—So what are the big issues?

—Love. With your moon in Libra, you're in the school of love.

Dan is at the kitchen sink in his boxers, mixing a pitcher of fruit punch. If it weren't so damn hot! It's six o'clock the morning of Christine's birthday, July in Montreal. Torture: like swimming around in a fish tank the size of a city. And because Christine's apartment is one floor above a Mexican restaurant, the humidity is also mixed with the smell of refried beans and charred chilies. Forget about air-conditioning. A neighbourhood ordinance prohibits portable units from marring the fronts of historic townhouses. As if that big neon yellow sombrero out on the sidewalk were any more dignified.

"Is it cherry?" Christine croaks from the doorway.

"Have you thought about what you want to go with your birthday revolver?" Dan asks, keeping it light. "A little leather holster, maybe?" He hates himself for sounding so goddamn chipper. Terminally perky. He wishes for the thousandth time that he were as funny as the rest of her friends.

"A weekend for two at the Yukon Hilton."

"A little out of my budget," Dan says, pouring fruit punch over a glass of ice. Everything is out of his budget. He was fired from his job last week. He got his boss to call it a lay-off—like Christine's—so he could collect unemployment. But the firm has never been busier. He's been taking too much time off, too many personal days. The truth is, the firm was just getting too busy to keep him on. Deadwood. He understands. He would have done the same thing in his boss' position.

"I'm serious," Christine says, examining her astrological chart, now posted on the refrigerator. She traces the magic-marker vectors of blue and red and green with her finger. "Let's at least go to a hotel downtown. The Queen Elizabeth. I'll put it on my credit card. I just want a good night's sleep. I'm convinced heaven is an eighteen-degree room. We could invite Claude over. Mary Margaret, maybe. Have some room service."

"Isn't that a little optimistic—a good night's sleep—regardless of where you are?"

"Tonight's the third night. I'll only throw up once or twice, tops."

Dan shrugs. He's stopped trying to reason with her. He has long ago lost his sense of reasonable boundaries. "We'll put it on my Visa," he says, forcing a smile. "It's your birthday, after all." He's not even sure if there is room on his Visa. Or his American Express. He's never been this strapped for money.

Christine smiles, there's a look of mischief on her face. The first he's seen since they stole a silver samovar from the Queen Elizabeth during the swing ball—just to see if they could get away with it. She told the doorman it was a family heirloom.

"Don't get mad at me, okay?" she says. "Just listen. I called MasterCard a couple of days ago. I asked them what happens—you know, theoretically—when a cardholder dies suddenly. They told me they're insured for that. When the estate can't pay off the bill, they don't go after the next of kin. They just take it as a loss. It's all calculated in the annual fees we pay."

"What are you saying?"

She begins to giggle. "I'm saying, let's put it on my MasterCard."

They both have a good laugh and a glass of fruit punch.

—Hmm. Mars is on your Venus in August.

—What's that mean?

—Chaotic aspects in the house that rules romance, partnership.

—What kind of chaos?

—I'd say you tend to choose romantic partners who typically take more than they give. And with your moon in Libra, it looks like you need the nurturing. Are you romantically involved?

—No. No, I'm not.

—See how Venus is aspected at twenty-five degrees Cancer?

—Yeah, so?

—Breaking from the past. I'd say you'll soon be breaking from the past.

Christine's parents call while they are getting dressed, packing an overnight bag. She's chipper with them. Perky. Everything's fine. Her parents are staunch Catholics from Sherbrooke. They still haven't gotten used to Dan answering the phone. People will think you're living together.

Living in sin. The very thought makes Dan laugh out loud. Sleeping together is such a thrill: Christine's utter stillness followed by incessant tossing and turning, then utter stillness again before she erupts into a jagged scream. And those two nights following her Thursday chemo treatment. Bed sweats. Sobbing fits. Hour after hour of purging chemicals pumped into her veins, poisons intended to make her well.

But everything seems crazy to Dan these days. Like the doctor who treated Christine's sprained ankle telling her she would need to be on crutches for at least six weeks—two weeks longer than she is projected to live. Crazy. Or Christine refusing to wear a flesh-coloured ace bandage because her flesh is nowhere near the right colour. And what about yesterday, when Christine asked a nurse during chemo to page the foot doctor because her ankle was beginning to swell? The nurse was forced to admit he'd died the night before in his sleep. It was all very sudden, she said: a heart attack.

Dan's parents wonder why they haven't met this Christine yet. Things must be serious, if they've moved in together.

Dan stuffs his bathing suit into Christine's duffel. He has no idea whether the Queen Elizabeth has a pool. Living in sin. Christine insists on making love once a week. Every Saturday night, about an hour after the dinner dishes have been done. Dan dreads these sexual encounters. It upsets him that Christine pencils them in on the Hello Kitty calendar next to the astrological chart on the fridge. But her chemo schedule leaves little room for spontaneity. And he knows how important it is to go through the motions. It's the only thing left, according to Christine, separating her from the produce at the IGA.

They have very unsafe sex now. This also upsets Dan. It upsets him because he finds it exciting, fucking with complete abandon. After all they've been through, it's the only way he could get an erection. Little deaths. It's been about a month since Christine told him to forget about the condom. "Live a little," she laughed one night when he was getting ready to enter her. And when he came, he was strangely comforted, comforted by the thought of pumping a little life into her.

Now, when she clutches him, her thin legs wrapped around his waist, he wonders. Why does she continue to hang on to this terrible life with such ferocity? He looks for answers in her eyes, but they are never open at the moment of climax. Her teeth are clenched and her eyes are squeezed shut. He wonders what she sees with her eyes shut. He wonders what she sees when she opens them again. She used to chatter the entire way through sex. Now you'd need to hold a mirror under her nose. She told him one weekend, at her family's cabin in Vermont—an eternity ago, it seems—that he was fucking a corpse. Now he too keeps his eyes shut while they're having sex.

—Neptune, here at the top of your chart, is your guiding planet, your guiding star. Neptune is a nebulous planet ruling the occult, things that can't be seen.

—I'm sorry; I don't mean to laugh. Go on.

—Well, Neptune rules your life mission.

—Which is?

—Which is to experience a whole lot of different things; to learn from strangers—in odd moments, in odd places.

—You mean I'm going to meet someone tall, dark and handsome?

—Well. Neptune is in Scorpio. And Scorpio rules passion. You're passionate about this life, about this mission. Pay close attention to your run-ins. What's wrong?

—Nothing. Yes, you're right; I'm passionate about this life.

—Wait. Are you crying?

***

Dan and Christine are waiting for the next bus downtown. Between them, they have pooled together change for two fares. Both are completely out of cash; Christine lives nowhere near an ATM machine. She stares off down the street, balancing on her crutches. Her short skirt and t-shirt reveal bone-white legs, too much skin for legs as translucent as that. At least an Expos cap covers the bald patches on her scalp; a pair of sunglasses hides how much the whites of her eyes have yellowed.

"Here comes one," she says.

"Oh shit," he says.

"Now what?"

"How are you going to make the steps?" It hasn't occurred to him until now that there are several steps up into the bus. "Maybe we should just hail a cab. We can have the driver pull up to the first ATM on the way to the hotel."

"Don't be absurd. The bus is right here. I'll manage."

She doesn't manage. The bus is packed with people headed downtown. A half-dozen have to step out to let people off. Then they jam themselves back on. No one is willing to clear the handrail so Christine can pull herself up into the vehicle. The driver shouts at her to either get on or step down. Finally, a pregnant woman offers her hand. Between Dan pushing from behind and the pregnant woman pulling from the front, they are able to hoist Christine inside. There are no seats. The pregnant woman tells them she's been standing since Park Extension. She says it loud enough that two younger women, college students, vacate nearby seats. All the men seem to be staring intently out the windows.

Dan seats himself and motions for Christine to sit on his lap. She looks as though she may faint. Or worse, throw up. She falls asleep instantly, with her arms around his neck. She is snoring; drooling a bit on his collar. Happy birthday to you ... The rocking motion of the bus causes Dan to nod off as well. Stops go by.

Christine screams. It takes a moment for Dan to realize what has happened. At first he thinks the scream is part of his dream. Then he thinks they are in bed, that this is just one of her nightly outbursts. Finally he understands. Someone has kicked her sprained foot. He can tell by the way she jerks it in from the aisle.

"Jesus Christ, it has a big red ace bandage on it!" she howls, not sure of her assailant. "What are you—fucking blind?"

"Why yes. I am. I'm very sorry." The man who answers is tall and wearing dark glasses, carrying a cane. A blind man.

Christine bursts into tears.

There is nothing Dan can do except hold her. What else can he do?

Mise en Abîme

His mother was clearing canning jars out of the root cellar when she found the first bottle. It was covered in dust, but she knew what it was. She didn't need the glare of a forty-watt bulb to tell her: Jim Beam, eighty proof, about a third full. Her arm jerked back, as if she'd discovered a snake dozing there in the cool damp. Her elbow struck one of the shelves behind her and she saw stars. Two-thirds empty, more like.

Her ears were not ringing; that was the telephone in the kitchen. She did not race upstairs to answer it. She did not place the bottle in one of the many trash bags or moving boxes at her feet. She did not rub her elbow to feel better. Instead, she began a search for the truth there in the half-light. She knocked over ancient jars of stewed tomatoes and wax beans in her haste. She broke a broom by poking its handle behind the furnace. She shone a flashlight along the floor beams above her until the batteries died. She wasn't dismantling thirty years of her life now. She was ransacking it.

She set all of the bottles down on her kitchen table: Jim Beam, Johnny Walker, Jack Daniels. She slumped into one of the matching maple chairs. She couldn't move after that; it was as if the clock over the sink were ticking away the minutes of another afternoon—an afternoon nine years ago—when another bottle of Jim Beam sat on that very table, separating her from her husband.

Watching him crush a cigarette out in an ashtray full of filters. Waiting for him to speak. You knew I liked my whiskey the day you

84

met me, he says, exhaling blue smoke. I didn't realize you would always choose it over me and the kids, she retorts. You're talking crazy, he says, where will you go? I'm not going anywhere, she informs him, you are—I packed your things, they're out on the porch. The clock above the sink, ticking. Nine minutes past the hour. What if I promise to stop, he says, less sure of himself now; what if I never take another drop? That's up to you, she says, it's too late to be doing it for me. I'm past loving you.

The jangle of the phone again. She sat motionless, letting it ring. Probably her daughter, wanting to know how the packing was going, or what sort of casserole to bring to supper tonight. She counted the rings— nine—waiting for silence. (She had never gotten around to installing the answering machine her kids had chipped in for one Christmas. She had never really needed it; she had always been there whenever they had called.) Her husband had cried that other time. He had emptied the bottle into the sink. He had taken her upstairs and made love to her. And she had never tasted Jim Beam on his breath again. He had begun showing up for dinner on time, he had stopped haunting the Canadian Club after work, stopped carousing with his brothers and cousins on the weekends. It had been hell that first year—he'd been so withdrawn and short-tempered—but eventually he had mellowed into the quiet, gentle man she had always assumed she'd married.

She stood. She would not call her daughter back. She would be seeing her at the nursing home in about an hour anyway. Instead she went to the phone and dialed her eldest son's number. He had promised to drive down to the farm after his office hours at the college, to help her with the rest of the packing. She desperately needed to know that he would show up. She needed him there—to see these bottles, to bear witness. To tell her what to think.

Her eldest son did not feel like thinking today. He found himself taking inventory of the glass-topped coffee table: oversize brass alarm clock (nine minutes before the hour), African violet in need of dusting, decorator box of tissues. How many of this woman's patients, he wondered, actually made use of the tissues? No way of telling from where he sat; the dispenser top only offered one jaunty tissue at a time. He would have to pick the box up and weigh it in his hand to know for sure. And if he were actually going to reveal he wasn't dredging up painful memories in this silence, he'd rather pinch dead blossoms off the plant.

"Have things improved between you and your wife?" his therapist prompted, after a furtive glance at the alarm clock.

He shrugged.

"You weathered last week's little reoccurrence?"

"I guess."

She scribbled something on her steno pad. "You seem a little detached today."

Reaching up to take the hand of an angel fluttering over his bed. Letting her lead him to the open window. Together they fly out into the night, soar over his family's farm. Above it all, the barn and pastures and woodlot seem surprisingly beautiful. Even the derricks of the quarry where his father and grandfather work look majestic rising up out of great hills of discarded granite at the rose-tinted horizon. But then he feels a tug on his arm, one that grows urgent in its insistence. Not his guardian angel after all. His mother, waking him in the middle of the night. Just leave him there this time, he groans; I've got a big French test tomorrow. I won't sleep, she says, I'll worry all night he's killed somebody driving himself home. So he climbs out of his warm bed. He shucks a pair of jeans and a sweatshirt over his pajamas with his mother watching from the edge of darkness. Together they tiptoe through the kitchen, and he notices she has finally cleared his father's uneaten plate from the table. The Chevy is already running in the yard. His mother drives to the Canadian Club, complaining the entire way how cheated she feels out of a life. She asks him yet again whether she should just pack his father's things and set them out on the porch. But he knows she won't. She will merely make him, her eldest son, fetch his father out of the bar. She will wait in the parking lot as he, with the help of the bartender, drags his father wounded soldier-style past grinning uncles and cousins while his father mumbles to anyone who will listen how his youngest son is twice the baseball player his eldest ever dreamed of being. Needless to say, he will not do well on his French test the next morning. The words won't come. It will be too hard, in the hushed quiet of the classroom, to keep awake.

The tick of the brass alarm clock on the table. Time nearly up. He pulled a tissue from the box and another sprang up to replace it. He pretended to blow his nose. "Detached," he said. "Three words you can make from detached are hate and ache and cheat."

His therapist encouraged him to take his thoughts a little deeper.

His thoughts: out of hate, tea or hat; out of ache, ace; out of cheat, heat or eat. "Death," he said. "You can also make the word death, I guess."

His mother arrived late for her weekly visit to the nursing home—so late, in fact, that she discovered her father-in-law's room empty. She found him in the sun room, hunched over in a wheelchair, staring out the window. Her daughter had obviously arrived some time ago; she was in mid-conversation with the attending nurse over the old man's head. Her daughter was telling the nurse that retirement from the quarry wouldn't be an easy adjustment for her father; he had worked so damn hard all his life. He would have to find himself some sort of hobby when he got to Florida or he'd drive her poor mother crazy.

She faked a cough, to let her daughter and the nurse know she was there.

"Where were you?" her daughter asked, utterly unconcerned that she had been caught gossiping. "I called and called. The phone rang off the hook."

"Must have been in the cellar," she replied. "How is Pépère today?"

"About the same," the nurse said, patting the old man's shoulder. "Aren't you, sweetie?" The old man, were he in his right mind, would have found such familiarity from someone so young outrageously disrespectful.

She perched on the edge of the orange vinyl sofa opposite the wheelchair, so that her eyes could be at the same level as her father-in-law's. "This'll be my last visit for a while," she said.

"You don't have to shout, Ma," her daughter said. "He isn't hard of hearing."

She ignored this. It had been years since the old man had actually spoken to her during her weekly visit—a man of few words to begin with—but today she needed to know she was getting through. She needed him to understand he would probably never see her again. "The kids'll still be by every week," she said. She looked to her daughter for confirmation; her daughter shrugged. "My husband was so sorry he couldn't come today," she lied. "But it's his last day at the quarry. They're giving him a little party. He expects he'll get the same gold watch you did." If only the old man would nod or blink. Anything.

"I'll get him a nice glass of juice," the nurse said.

"I go with you," her daughter said. "I could use a cup of coffee. Want one, Ma?"

She shook her head. Her daughter and the nurse strolled off together, happy to continue their chat. Good. She was desperate to tell her father-in-law her secret. But there were nine others in the room. Among them another old man complaining about his aches and pains to a middle-aged son; an old lady giggling while her granddaughter, a school girl, spun her wheelchair around and hopped onto the rear axle for the ride.

Picking bugle beads off the sleeve of her wedding gown. Fretting that no one is mixing. Her new husband's family drink and joke in French on one side of the Canadian Club, her own family stare, arms crossed in disapproval, from the other. Weddings are solemn occasions where her family comes from. You eat a quiet meal, you make a quiet toast. You wish the happy couple many children, and you go home. But her new husband's relatives have brought guitars and banjos. The men tune up while their wives push back the tables. Where is her new husband? He's taking up a cousin's fiddle. His cheeks are flushed with too much champagne, his hair has fallen over his eyes. Her breath catches—he's that handsome—as the Canadians begin to dance. Her new father-in-law rushes up. He takes her hand and bows, pantomiming his invitation to join the reel. (He understands English better than he speaks it.) He smells of whiskey and mischief. She tells him she doesn't know how to clog. He drags her to the dance floor anyway. They join the swirl and he begins to spin her around the room. They dance through one song and then another. When finally she begs him to stop—she's feeling dizzy from all that spinning—he offers her the silver flask from his hip pocket. She takes a small sip, feeling welcomed. She tells him she really ought to be getting back to her own family. But another reel is forming, and they join it.

A harrumph of disapproval. "Somebody's going to get hurt," her daughter said, blowing into a Styrofoam cup of coffee and nodding at the spinning wheelchair. "She's old enough to know better than that."

The school girl? The lady in the wheelchair? "I can't stay much longer," she told her daughter. "I haven't started the pies yet for tonight."

Her daughter shrugged. "I'll follow you back to the farm," she said. "I can do some of the packing up while you bake. You don't have to do everything alone, you know."

She didn't want her daughter to see the bottles sitting in the middle of the kitchen table. She wanted her daughter to believe that everything was fine, that her parents were about to embark on the adventure of a lifetime. Her daughter was always saying how proud she was that her parents were one of the last happily married couples left in town.

Her eldest son pulled into the parking lot of the nursing home. He couldn't stay long; he shouldn't even have come. He should be at his mother's, helping her pack. He should be holding office hours—his sophomores had a mid-term coming up. But his mother had practically begged him. She was making a big dinner for the immediate family tonight, for his father's last day of work. So he had forced himself to cross campus after therapy and tape a note to his door: Office hours canceled. Family emergency.

"You just missed your mom and your sister," the attending nurse said. She was leading him down the corridor to the old man's room. The corridor smelled of piss and pine detergent.

"I'll be seeing them later," he said.

"Big party, I hear," the nurse said, smiling.

"How's my Pépère today?" he asked. It wasn't going to be a big party at all. Just the immediate family. The first time they had all been in the same room together for years.

"About the same," she said. She pushed open the door to his room.

His grandfather was sitting fully dressed at the edge of his bed, poised as though he were waiting. His hat rested on the neat coverlet beside him. The old man looked up when he heard the door. A shadow of disappointment crossed his face.

"*Comment-allez vous, monsieur?*"

"*J'attends le bon Dieu,*" his grandfather replied. "*Entre-temps, asseyez-vous, jeune-homme.*" He was invited to take a seat. The nurse left them alone.

They only spoke in French, now. The old man insisted on the formal you. He did not understand that this pleasant young man, speaking with a distinguished European accent, was his grandson. As far as he knew, his grandchildren didn't speak French. He had no idea the eldest boy had gone off to college and gotten a French degree, had written his master's thesis in Paris, had married a French woman, had gotten a professorship at the state university.

"I must warn you, sir," the old man confided, "our visit will have to be brief today. My son will be interrupting us at any moment to collect me."

"Is that so?" he said. To his knowledge, his father had never once visited the old man at the nursing home.

"Yes. My son is finally taking my advice. We are returning to Quebec."

"Just the two of you?"

"Yes."

"What about his wife?"

The old man shrugged.

Walking the property line, mending fences. His father and grandfather speak only in French (a language he has not been taught since his mother doesn't speak it). He concentrates on the sounds. French is the language of men; and he needs to learn it. Which are the words about co-workers down at the quarry? Which are the ones about relatives back in Canada? Which are about unathletic eldest sons? Often, the two men don't use words at all. They use an even more mystifying language of silence and gesture. Nod of head meaning: hold that length of barbed wire taut; angle of elbow meaning: steady that post with fieldstones. Which gesture signifies it's time to pull the flask out of the hip pocket? He is thirsty too, but there is nothing for a boy to drink. So he takes himself off to a friendlier place, to California, where the focus of attention is on him for a change. He surrounds himself with smiling blond people who are never in bad moods. He pretends he is one of the Monkees— Mick—and he gets so wrapped up in his madcap adventures with Davy and Mike and Pete, so intent on pleasing his adoring fans, that he begins to play the guitar and strut around his father's hayfield. Until his father barks—in English—Stop acting like a girl. Until his grandfather mumbles something in French and they both laugh. He stops playing the air guitar, he stops dancing. He doesn't have the words to explain that he isn't acting like a girl; he's acting like a Monkee.

His mother stopped rolling out pie crust and sat in the nearest chair. She hadn't gotten the lard right, and the dough was brittle. Her eyes wandered to the dusty bottles on the kitchen table, in among the cartons of eggs and milk, canisters of flour and lard. Dinner would never be ready at six-thirty. She hadn't even started on the roast. Where was her eldest son? She feared she would not be able to move until he arrived.

A quick rap on the back door, someone was letting himself in. Someone calling, It's me, Ma. She sighed. Not her eldest son; her youngest.

"You're early," she said.

"Need anything from town?" her youngest said, taking the chair opposite hers. He was a UPS man and he often stopped in, if his route took him by the farm.

"No," she said. "—Yes, I do. Lemons for iced tea. The ones I have aren't nice. Cup of coffee?"

"I'm all set," he said. A moment of silence. Something was on his mind, something was troubling him. The bottles! He was too afraid to bring them up, too afraid to ask what they meant—what they were doing in this house after nine years.

"I delivered *mon oncle*'s new milking machine this morning," he said. "He seemed a little upset he wasn't asked to Dad's party tonight."

"It isn't a party," she said.

"You know what I mean," he said. "The Canadians were all expecting to be asked over—to wish Dad well. Maybe you should call *ma tante* and invite everyone for coffee and dessert. She'd spread the word. They'd bring stuff. It's not too late for me to swing by the bakery, if you want."

"It's not a party."

"I think Dad would like it."

What was wrong with him? Couldn't he see the goddamn bottles sitting there: Jim Beam, Johnny Walker, Jack Daniels. Three unexpected guests for dinner were about all she could handle. "If they want a party, they can throw one," she said.

"Don't get upset," he said. "It was just a thought. Look, I've got to go. What time do you want us? Six-thirty?"

"Better make it seven."

Waiting as the house party rages around her. Listening for that moment when she can finally hear the kitchen clock ticking. She hasn't moved from her chair since setting out the whiskey and coffee cups and poundcake. She hasn't spoken in hours; her husband's relatives have abandoned English. She hates Friday nights most of all: the steady drinking of hard liquor out of tiny chipped-beef jars, the chain-smoking of cigarettes that fill her house with thick blue smoke, the forced laughter over dirty-sounding jokes she doesn't understand, the singing of songs she doesn't understand. The longer the evening wears on, the more morose the Canadians get. Tears fill their eyes, a longing for home. Their tones turn somber, the pauses between stories and songs grow longer and longer until finally—when you can hear the clock ticking—they all sit in silence with their hands braced on their knees, staring down at the linoleum. A high, shrill shout. Her eldest boy, standing before them in his pajamas, hands on hips, hair on end. Don't you people have children to get home to? The Canadians stare at him, stunned. Children are to be seen and not heard. He glares back, stamps his foot. A cousin or brother begins to laugh. The rest join in, a little uncertainly at first, but then uproariously. Kids say the damnedest things. She stands. She takes her eldest son's shoulder. She leads him by the hand back to bed. She tucks him in, kisses him on the forehead, reassures him they will all be gone soon. And even as she speaks the Canadians are shuffling their chairs back, making the good-bye sounds. See you down at the Club. My place next week.

The grind of gears out in the yard. She stood. She watched her youngest son drive off in his truck. She fetched a knife from the drawer and began scraping pie crust off the table. He wasn't coming. He had promised, and he had broken his promise again. She threw the knife on the table and sat back down. She felt so cheated, cheated out of a life. Should she pack her husband's things? Should she leave them out on the porch? She didn't know. She needed to wait now, wait for him to get home from his last day of work, his pocket heavy with a gold watch, to tell her what to think.

Her eldest son ordered another Jim Beam from the barmaid. He had dropped by the Canadian Club on his way to the farm, for a little courage. Long night ahead. The barmaid brought his whiskey right away, smiling too much, lingering too long. "I'm sorry," she said, "I was just struck by your eyes. They're so big and sad."

"You can thank my parents for that," he said, toasting her.

She smiled, not understanding. A middle-aged man came in. That made nine total customers in the bar. Nine was a curious number, he told the barmaid. When you multiplied nine by any other number other than zero the sum of the digits in the resulting number totaled nine or a number whose total digits, when added together, would total nine.

I'll be right back," the barmaid said, drifting off to take the new customer's order. "Don't go away."

Mature women tended to hit on him. (His wife was older by nine years.) He looked like the type who would never hurt them; the sensitive, artistic type who needed taking care of. He had not yet learned how to tell them up-front they were wrong. Why he was in therapy: to learn how to say no. He was not the type of man who needed women to protect him. He was, in fact, the type who always hurt women.

How many times had he dragged his father out of this place? What if he walked through that door right now? What if the old man was stopping by the Club with his brothers and cousins to celebrate his last day of work? Would his eldest son offer to buy him a drink? What would that be like—to shoot the shit with his old man over a quick whiskey? His father hadn't taken a drop in nine years. He'd just stopped one day. No AA, no twelve-step, no nothing. Just lost his taste for it, he'd said. These days, he didn't have much to say at all.

He raised his glass to drain it. There was a long mirror behind the bar. He watched himself drinking. And because there was also a wall of mirrors behind him, blocking off the bathrooms, he could see the reflection of the bar's mirror and the reflection of a man in it—himself—draining his glass. And behind that man, another man in another mirror, drinking. And so on, into infinity. A phenomenon the French called *mise en abîme*. He'd learned that in Paris. Thrown into the abyss.

He squinted at himself in the mirror, looking into his own eyes to see if he could see what women saw. What men saw.

Waking to a pair of bloodshot eyes glowering down at him. Gagging on a blast of sour whiskey breath. His father cuffs him in the ear—not hard, really; just enough to make his point. If you ever embarrass me in front of my family like that again, he says, I'll kill you. You hear me? His father staggers off to bed, without waiting for an answer. He nods, anyway. And he waits. He waits until he hears the creak of his parents' bedsprings. He waits through their murmurings and through the following silence until he hears his father snoring. He crawls out of bed then, and creeps to the kitchen. He stands on a chair and opens the cabinet above the refrigerator. He takes out the bottles of Jim Beam, Johnny Walker and Jack Daniels. He gathers them up in his arms and makes his way to the basement. He begins hiding bottles: one in the root cellar, another behind the

94

furnace, another in the floor beams above his head. His father won't remember how much he and his family have drunk that night. And his mother will just assume the Canadians have taken the bottles home with them. He will empty them later—tomorrow—when no one is around. He will bury them in the back pasture.

The scrape of an empty shot glass across the zinc of the bar. *Cadavres*, the French word for empty bottles. He signaled for the barmaid and paid her. With the coins of his change, he went to the phone booth. He did not dial his mother's number. He would not be calling her to apologize for not turning up that afternoon to help her pack. He would not be warning her that he intended to skip her little dinner party tonight. Instead, he dialed his own number, hoping his wife was home from work. He got their answering service—his own voice—apologizing to him for not being there, reassuring him that he would call himself right back, if he left his number and a brief message. At the tone, he told himself that something had come up. He would explain everything later. But he shouldn't worry. With any luck he would be home by just about nine.

We're from HQ and We're Here to Help You

CASTLES ARE MERE BLURS on the autobahn. Jeanette, my new boss, is explaining how the body derives equal amounts of energy from sleep and food. We are almost an hour late for a meeting in Heidelberg where I will be introduced as the new director of marketing worldwide—in yesterday's suit and tie. Neither of us has a single euro for this astronomical cab ride.

Jeanette hands me half a bar of duty-free Swiss chocolate. Blood red fingernails. She has scheduled ten such meetings in as many countries over the next nine days. Jeanette's opinion: sleeping at night is out of the question, if we hope to have any fun. She decides we'll simply double our intake of food. Eat a meal every four hours, take catnaps on planes. Rumour has it she was once a dancer for Les Grands Ballets Canadiens—or was that Cirque du Soleil? Either way, her legs certainly turned heads at the Frankfort airport this morning. I have long thought she looks like a movie-star princess.

In flawless German, Jeanette asks the cab driver if it's at all possible to go faster. The driver answers no. I am inclined to believe him, though Jeanette frowns. She whispers that she won't sleep with Germans for that very reason—their cautious nature. Squinting at me, she assesses my probable ethnic origin. She says we shall have to do something about my clothes when we get to a civilized airport. Milan perhaps. Or Paris.

Yesterday, I was a lowly marketing analyst in Montreal. But my company—an international tour operator—completely reorganized itself while I was at lunch. As soon as I got back, I was congratulated on my promotion and referred to Human Resources. There I was handed a Lufthansa ticket, my passport (kept on hand in the safe by corporate policy), a carry-on bag with matching shaving kit from the executive supply room, and the following e-mail: Meet me tomorrow Frankfort airport. Aeroflot flt 6767, arr 09.15 h. Looking forward to having you. Jeanette.

Yesterday, Jeanette was in Moscow. She was buying up every available hotel bed for Easter and the summer season. She was also looking for office space close to the Kremlin. It is no secret that sales for her latest tour, The New Democratic Russia, have gone through the roof. Jeanette's Russian is apparently excellent. I imagine her in a smoky room, hunkered around a table with mono-eyebrowed men, making deals over shot after shot of vodka. Rumour has it Jeanette will do anything—anything—to get what she wants.

The driver informs us we have another ten minutes before Heidelberg. Jeanette suggests we use the delay to our advantage by deciding what we shall actually do at these meetings. She suggests I take notes. Meeting Agenda: 1) coffee & rolls, introductions; 2) Jeanette to explain reorganization (lots of enthusiasm!); 3) me to explain plans for radical improvements to sales & marketing (keep short); 4) lunch out somewhere nice, coffee back at office; 5) Jeanette to ask how we can help them when we're back at HQ (pretend to write every suggestion down); 6) have a cab for airport waiting by 3 p.m. sharp; 7) important! kisses good-bye on cheeks (2), every woman, all countries except: Holland (3), Denmark (1), England (0).

Jeanette asks if there are any questions. I have just one: my plans for radical improvements to sales and marketing. But it's too late. The cab is pulling up in front of a building where our corporate logo blazes in neon above the door. Jeanette negotiates with the driver to pay half the fare in euros, the rest in Swiss francs (she was in Geneva just before Moscow); the exchange rate for the francs to be rounded-up to the nearest euro from this morning's London *Times*. I am to tip in U.S. dollars, not Canadian. Once on the sidewalk, Jeanette advises me: keep it short.

***

Our routine varies little from country to country. At ten a.m., we take our seats at the head of a conference table laden with coffee (tea in Ireland), breakfast rolls (croissants in Paris) and sparkling water (*sin gaz* in Madrid). Between us, a note pad. At the top, the name of the country (easy to forget because all the meetings are in English). Next to it, a tiny diagram of the conference table. As introductions are made, we write the first two letters of each person's name in the appropriate position around our diagram. An asterisk goes next to Who's-In-Charge. This system works well. By Austria, we rarely draw a blank as to Who's-In-Charge.

Jeanette stands at a flip-chart. She sketches a complicated series of inter-connected boxes, representing the reorganization. Very little is clear, except that her box is at the top. She is nonetheless enthusiastic: all the new layers of management have been added to improve the quality of our services worldwide. We have a short bathroom break during which Jeanette returns only the most frantic of her telephone messages. She is always clutching an impressive thick, pink stack. Back at the flip-chart, Jeanette points out my box again and turns the floor over to me.

I tell them: Work is underway on a comprehensive product analysis to identify new sales opportunities across all market segmentations. Once identified, these opportunities will be converted to empirically tested media strategies for newsprint, direct mail—maybe even television. All programs will be closely monitored for effectiveness, with feedback from them playing an integral role. Basically, I tell them anything I can remember from the Intro to Marketing course I took at McGill. I conclude with an assurance that my team of experts will help tailor these radically improved sales and marketing plans to the specific needs of (a quick glance at the note pad) all of you working so diligently in Belgium. Applause.

When I sit back down, Jeanette squeezes my wrist under the table. She asks if there are any questions before we move on to other business. There never are; though at that moment, I often feel like blurting out the truth, There is no plan! I'm just a lowly analyst! I'm no marketing guru! But I don't. Because at that moment, I usually have a hard-on.

We break for lunch. Jeanette returns a few more phone calls while a secretary arranges sufficient cabs to take us to a nice restaurant. Once there, Jeanette orders several bottles of wine to get everyone a little drunk. They are quite subdued by the time we get around to asking what we can do for them as soon as we get back to HQ.

We only ever sleep on planes.

It is early evening when the flight attendant rocks us awake to prepare us for landing in our next country. After the usual haggling with our cab driver in mismatched currencies, we check into our hotel rooms. Then the hardest moment of the day: staring lustfully at a virginal bed, knowing it will remain pristine however much I long to defile it before checking out. I splash water on my face. I know Jeanette is waiting for me in the lobby.

We always end up at a restaurant where the maître d' rushes over to Jeanette and kisses her on the cheek. We never order from menus; delicious food and wine just appear at appropriate intervals. We rarely ever pay. Jeanette invariably suggests over coffee that we meet a special friend of hers, someone she hasn't seen in ages. So we take a cab across town either to a little bar with atmosphere or a trendy nightclub with a line out the door (which, of course, we skirt). Her special friends are without exception middle-aged businessmen with mustaches. They all have dual citizenship, both in Switzerland and wherever they are actually from. Over whiskey, I hear about fantastic political scandals or encroaching world events months before they will become common knowledge. I watch Jeanette hang on their every word. I watch her place her hand on their wrists whenever they whisper things to her in languages I don't understand. I get very drunk and find myself longing for those cool, smooth hotel sheets, or for my own bed back in Montreal.

If we are at a nightclub, we eventually dance. If we are at a small bar, we take the special friend's Mercedes to a place where we can dance.

When I'm on the dance floor with Jeanette, I don't care that I've never been able to hear the beat of music. I no longer think about the brink of physical exhaustion. I no longer worry about such rich food in such large quantities. I no longer fret about these mustachioed men. And I no longer care what my plans are for radical changes to sales and marketing. I am mercifully focused on dancing; on Jeanette, the former ballerina, who sways and dips and pirouettes to the bass rhythms of music so loud it changes our heartbeats. I find myself anticipating that delicious moment, just before dawn, when she will grip my wrist with those blood red fingernails and shout into my ear, I'm so glad to have you, Dan.

Pegasus's Missing Wing

IT's ABOUT to happen again.

This time it's the man over in the cookbook section. He's pretending to read a recipe, but his eyes are boring into me over the top of *Lord Krishna's Cuisine*. My wife Chantelle hasn't noticed him yet; she's too busy greeting customers. Why now, when we've finally gotten it together to open our own health food store? Everything's perfect: the oak floors are gleaming, the shelves are all neatly stocked, the bulk bins are brimming, the aisles are mobbed. Maybe he'll decide he's wrong. Maybe he'll just go away and let us have our big day without spoiling it.

He slides *Lord Krishna* back onto the shelf. He starts to circle his way over, checking out the yoga mats, tasting the organic wine, sniffing a cantaloupe to test its ripeness. I try not to panic. They always look so familiar when this happens. Then again, they're invariably gay men in their forties. Finally he steps up to the Customer Care desk where Chantelle and I have stationed ourselves for the day.

"Bonjour, can I help you find anything?" Chantelle says.

"No," he says. "—Yes, I have question. But it's not for you. It's for your colleague."

Close up, I see this man is different.

"What's up?" I say.

"You might find it embarrassing."

"He's not Ricky Bronco," she says. "If that's what you want to know."

The man turns crimson. "I'm sorry," he says. "I didn't think so. It's just that the resemblance is—well—amazing."

"You're not the first to make that mistake," Chantelle reassures him. "It happens all the time."

He takes a second look at me. He doesn't seem convinced.

"Ricky Bronco was his twin brother," she says.

"He's dead now," I say.

"Oh," the man says.

And then he just stands there.

"Is there anything else?" I ask. People are, after all, lining up behind him to congratulate us.

"Sorry," he says. "I sort of knew him. I taught in San Francisco for a while. At UCSF. Ricky was sort of a friend—well—more like an acquaintance, I guess."

"His real name was Sam," I say. "Sam McKeag. I'm Scott. This is my wife Chantelle."

"I'm Beller. I'm just in Montreal for a conference."

No one knows what to say next.

"Funny," he says, after a moment. "We actually spent a fair amount of time together, Ricky and I. But I didn't know he was a twin. And I definitely didn't know he was—"

"AIDS," I say. "That's what the Internet says."

"No one knows for sure," Chantelle adds. "He stormed off the set of his last movie and was never seen or heard from again."

"But it's pretty widely assumed he died under an assumed name in one of the Bay Area hospices," I say. "Just Google 'Ricky Bronco'. It's all there."

And it's true, anyone with a computer can piece together Sam's story. After a few years of hustling in Montreal, he took a Greyhound bus to San Francisco. He began hustling in the bars along Polk Street and met a gay porn producer, the one who first used him as an extra in an orgy scene. That led to a few cameo appearances in other films, steady work as a stunt dick and, eventually, stardom. He only ever topped; he never bottomed. He wasn't actually gay himself. He made gay porn because it paid three times better than straight porn.

A tear trickles down this manBeller's cheek. "Sorry," he mumbles, brushing it away. "I was just so thrilled to see you—him—again."

He keeps standing there.

"Maybe we could all get together for coffee sometime," Chantelle says. "Sam's life—his real life—is such a mystery to us."

"When?" the man says.

"We're a little crazed at the moment," I say.

Beller digs a card out of his wallet and hands it to me. He says he's staying at the Queen Elizabeth until Wednesday. He's free any night.

"Well, nice meeting you," I say. "Take care."

"We'll definitely call you," Chantelle says.

Finally Beller steps away from the counter. Finally he drifts out the door and down the street.

"Cuckoo!" I sing-song under my breath.

Chantelle snatches his card out of my hand. "Classics professor," she says. "God, the world is one weird place."

"I'd better get another tray of California rolls for the buffet table," I say.

"Isn't this great?" Chantelle says, waving Beller's card. "Someone who actually knew Sam. Maybe you can finally lay this obsession you have with your dead brother to rest."

"I'm not the one who's obsessed," I say. "You are."

Beller turns up at seven o'clock on the dot.

"What an interesting space," he says, when I let him in.

"It's going to be," I say. "We've got a long ways to go."

I show him around the ground floor: the living area, the dining area, the office space. I explain how we saved this old granite warehouse on the waterfront from the wrecking ball; how we've been restoring it, bit by creaky bit, ourselves.

"I wanted to apologize," Beller says, suddenly, "for embarrassing you in your store the other day."

"I guess I'm used to it," I say.

"Odd thing to get used to—being mistaken for an icon of gay pornography."

"I didn't even get what was going on at first," I say. "Why guys were constantly sidling up to me and offering me fifty bucks to see my dick. Until I finally asked one of them who this Ricky Bronco was. I was completely mortified. I scrambled around to every porn shop in the Village to buy up any videos featuring him on the cover. But then I had no idea what to do with them. I didn't want them stacked around my apartment, didn't want to leave them out on the sidewalk at trash day ..."

"Your wife seems pretty okay with the whole thing now," Beller says.

"Are you kidding? She'd inform everyone I was a porn star's identical twin if I'd let her."

Beller laughs. I tell him Chantelle's in the kitchen with our son, Max. We're making lasagna for dinner and we've opened a bottle of red. I ask him if he'd like a glass. He nods. I lead him down the hallway to the kitchen, and he laughs again. The hallway is lined with old porcelain toilets potted with palms.

Chantelle is at the butcher's block cranking whole-wheat pasta out of the extruder I got her for Christmas. "I'm so glad you could make it," she says to Beller.

"I'm Max!" Max calls from beneath the kitchen table.

"Our three-year-old," Chantelle says.

"Three going on thirteen," I say.

Beller crouches down. "Hi Max," he says.

"I'm very busy," Max says.

"So I see," he says. "You've got all sorts of animals under there with you."

"My Daddy made them for me. It's our farm."

"Scott's a total country boy at heart," Chantelle stage-whispers.

"I grew up on a dairy farm in Vermont," I say, pouring Beller a glass of cabernet.

"Ricky was raised on a farm?" Beller says.

I explain how Sam ran away from home when he was fifteen. One night he just stuffed all of his belongings into a pillowcase, I say, and climbed out his bedroom window. When he didn't turn up for the morning milking, it became pretty clear that he—and all the emergency money in the cookie jar—were gone for good.

"What did your parents do," Beller asks, "when they finally found out he was—?"

"The star of *Riding the Wild Bronco I* and *II*?" Chantelle says.

"Could you cool it?" I say, nodding down at Max.

"Oh, he doesn't understand," she says.

"There's only my father," I say, turning to Beller. "My mother died in a car accident when we were boys. My dad still doesn't know about Sam—or, at least I don't think he does. He's pretty old school. He doesn't own a PC or have Internet access, and he only ever uses the VCR we gave him to record reruns of *M*A*S*H*."

"You don't know what he rents at the local video store," Chantelle says.

I scoop Max up from the floor. "I think it's time for somebody's B - A - T - H." I motion for Chantelle to take him.

"I'm covered in flour," she says. "Why don't you guys take your wine upstairs. I'll get supper into the oven while you're putting the papoose down."

"Really?" I say, trying to catch her eye. "Doesn't it make more sense for me to take over the pasta-making while you bathe Max?"

"You don't mind, Beller, do you?" she says.

Beller shrugs uncertainly.

I don't press it. There's no reasoning with Chantelle when she's trying to make one of her points. I set Max down. "It's time to start corralling your animals back into the barn for the night," I tell him. Max sets to work gathering them into his red beach pail and Beller crouches down to help. Meanwhile I top up Beller's glass, then pour a massive one for myself. I hand the glasses to Beller and hoist Max onto my shoulders. I take them both up the back staircase to the loft level.

"Promise not to talk about anything juicy till you get back," Chantelle calls after us.

Promise.

I begin filling the tub for Max, making sure to squeeze lots of bubble bath into the stream of water. I ask Beller to fetch a pair of pajamas from the top dresser drawer of Max's room at the end of the hall. While he's gone, I quickly shuck Max out of his clothes and plop him into the suds so that, by the time Beller's back, about all you can see of him is his head and arms. Beller perches on the toilet as I start to wash Max's hair. Max asks Beller to hand over the tugboat. Beller looks around mystified. I explain it's the lump of hammered-together wood scraps in the toy crate beside him. He sets it gently on the surface of the water. Max explains to Beller that only the lucky animals in his red bucket will make it onto the deck. Each time I try to soap him up, he wriggles out of my hands then crows with delight.

"Settle down," I say. "You're soaking poor Mr. Beller."

Beller holds out the bucket for Max. "So which one's first to get a ride on the ark?" he says.

"It's a tugboat," Max says.

"Sorry," Beller says. "How silly of me."

"The elephant," Max says.

Beller fishes the elephant out of the bucket. Max asks for the giraffe. Beller hands it to him. I take advantage of this distraction to rinse my son's hair.

"Give me another animal," Max demands, pushing me away.

"Hey," I say. "What's the magic word?"

"Please," he drones.

Beller pulls an animal from the bucket: a winged horse, one of my first attempts. Awkwardly carved and ill-proportioned, scarred by many battles with life, stained with Max's fruity drool. One of the horse's wings is missing. The scar has been rubbed shiny from many fondlings.

"Pegasus!" Max cries, reaching for him eagerly.

I wait. I wait. I wait. An eon drags by as Beller contemplates the misshapen creature in his palm.

"What happened here?" he asks Max, pointing to the missing wing.

Max shrugs. "Nobody knows," he says.

Beller hands Max the horse as Chantelle calls up the stairwell: "Dinner's safely in the oven, guys. I'm putting veggies and dip on the table."

"I'll meet you downstairs," I tell Beller. "I'm just going to put this one to B - E - D."

"Yeah, okay," Beller says. He stands. His pants are stained with water and soap bubbles. "Good night, Max," he says.

"See you later alligator," Max says.

I wait to hear the clump of Beller's shoes down the back staircase before I pull the plug in the tub. Max stands, dripping with suds. I begin to squeegee them off with my hands until his bright pink, naked little body emerges. He laughs uproariously.

His tugboat has capsized and his animals are drowning.

When Max asks for a bedtime story, I tell him not tonight—Daddy and Mommy have company—though I'm desperate to crawl beneath the covers with him for another installment of *Winnie-the-Pooh*. Instead I place Pegasus under Max's pillow and kiss him goodnight. I put out the light. I wish my son sweet dreams.

After the salad, Beller begins his story. He had just moved to San Francisco and didn't know anyone. Horny, he had called one of the escort numbers in the back of the local gay rag and the porn star Ricky Bronco had turned up. Beller had thought he'd won the lottery. Unfortunately sex had pretty much been a disaster. Ricky admitted he was coked out of his mind and couldn't get hard. He apologized about the unprofessionalism—he'd had a really shitty day—and gave Beller his money back. It was raining buckets by then, so Beller offered him a beer. They got to chatting, and Ricky entertained him with card tricks and sleight-of-hand, peppering his performance with behind-the-scenes gossip about the porn stars he worked with. It was at that point he confided to Beller that he wasn't really into guys. This made Beller, absurd as it sounds, feel a lot better about the sex. It was still raining, so Beller made them both a tuna sandwich. They watched TV as they ate. Ricky fell asleep on the couch. After that, Ricky would turn up at Beller's apartment most rainy days. They watched a lot of TV together. Sometimes they made spaghetti or tacos—neither of them was much of a cook.

"Did you ever, you know, talk?" Chantelle asks Beller. She's a big talker.

"A little," Beller says.

"Any idea why he ran away from home?" she asks.

"He told me his father molested him," Beller says. "He said he couldn't take it any more so he split."

A moment of stunning silence.

"Sorry," Beller says.

Chantelle turns to me, alarmed.

"Never," I tell her. "Are you kidding? The only time I think Dad ever even hugged me was the day I left home to move here." More silence. "Oh come on!" I say to Chantelle. "You've met my father."

"Barely," she says. She turns to Beller. "Scotty doesn't really get along with his Dad. We see him at Thanksgiving and Max's birthday. I'm strictly forbidden to bring up the subject of Sam."

"He might have been lying," Beller says. "About the abuse, I mean. Ricky was a pathological liar."

Chantelle fetches the lasagna from the oven. I remind her to put the cobbler in. I open another bottle of wine. She brings the lasagna pan to the table and serves us each a piping square. It's way over-cooked. But we all pretend it's good.

"So you guys really were sort of friends," Chantelle prompts Beller.

"It was pretty one-sided," Beller says, staring into his picked-at plate of pasta. "He only turned up at my doorstep when he felt like it. Oh, I had his beeper number, but he didn't always answer my calls. I didn't even know where he lived."

"But you had probably made a life for yourself by then," I say. "Right?"

Beller sighs. He looks up. "By then I had my students. I was friendly with colleagues in my department. I met guys at the gym. I dated. But I still wasted a lot of time waiting around that apartment, hoping the doorbell might ring."

"Why?" Chantelle says. "Sounds like Ricky was kind of an asshole."

Beller considers this. "He was smart," he says. "Really smart. And curious. He was curious about everything—what I was teaching, what I was translating. Every once in a while I could convince him to go to a museum with me, or the ballet, or the opera. He loved sculpture, actually. We spent a lot of time at the De Young." Beller turns to me.

"Ricky whittled too," Beller says. "He was actually pretty good. I tried to convince him to take a course."

"Isn't the twin thing spooky?" Chantelle says, laying her hand over mine.

We all take a sip of wine.

"So what happened?" she asks. "Between the two of you?"

"I was giving a paper at a conference in Madison," Beller says. "Ricky was supposed to look after my place while I was away, water my plants. When I got back, he was gone. The TV and the stereo were gone, a bunch of other stuff was gone. I never saw him again. I don't think anybody did. He just vanished."

"How sad," Chantelle sighs.

"What about you two?" Beller says. "How did you meet?"

Chantelle tells him our story: that we were both working in the same health food store here in Montreal, that we moved to Quebec City for a while to manage a chain franchise, that we decided to get married when she got pregnant with Max, that we decided to return to Montreal to open our own place when the chain got bought out.

"And now I have to rescue that cobbler before it burns too," Chantelle says. She stands. She kisses me on the forehead. She makes for the kitchen.

Beller and I stare into the candle flames.

"I almost got away with it," I say.

"It broke my heart to find Pegasus missing. You carved him for me. He was my birthday present."

"I know."

We listen to Chantelle in the kitchen, getting the dessert together. I sip my wine. He sips his wine.

"Are you going to tell her?" I ask.

"No," he says. "Ricky's gone."

Gone and not gone. No one knows better than I: porn has an astonishingly long half-life. Especially now, with the Internet. Who knows how many ages will have to pass before anyone Googling Ricky Bronco—including my son—comes up with rodeo ponies instead of unspeakable acts?

Chantelle returns triumphant. The cobbler is perfect. She scoops out a big portion for each of us. She crowns each with a dollop of yogurt.

There's nothing I can do but scrape the yogurt aside and dig in.

Black Tie

ALISON'S HEART SINKS the moment she recognizes Guy, her daughter's ex-boyfriend, milling among the guests. She pretends she doesn't see his wave. Instead she air-kisses a business associate of her husband Wayne. How can Guy possibly think he is welcome at this rehearsal dinner? Alison only sent him a wedding invitation as a formality—and only because Michaela, her daughter, had insisted. That Guy has flown to Boston without any encouragement only confirms Alison's long-standing opinion: he was never bright enough for Michaela to begin with.

Alison steels herself. She will just have to ignore him. The mother of the bride has duties to perform on the eve of her only daughter's wedding. Alison must smile, air-kiss friends and relatives hello, grasp the hands of strangers. She must show the invited guests where to check their coats, guide them to the buffet, remind them about the open bar.

It's no use. Alison knows, with the certainty of an oncoming migraine, that everything is ruined now. It no longer matters that this elegant party, hosted by her three sisters, is at the Harvard Club; that every single forecast has pronounced it to be a perfect late-summer weekend; that the diamond tiara of Michaela's veil—Alison's special gift to her—will break into earrings, a brooch, and a pendant afterward; that Wayne has finally convinced the bishop, a golf buddy, to perform the ceremony himself at Trinity Church in Copley Square; that the reception tomorrow evening is being held at the Blaxton

Country Club—the *Blaxton* Club—because Wayne was its first African-American member in the late 'eighties. None of it matters, none of it. This can never be the wedding of Alison's dreams. All of her memories of it will now have to include the idea of Guy Blanchard.

All that matters to Alison is a cool glass of chardonnay, one she has promised herself she will not have.

Please let this be a stress headache.

"Guy!" Michaela calls from across the room. Alison watches her daughter break away from a group of Dartmouth friends to give him a hug. "I'm so glad you're here," Michaela cries. "I was worried you wouldn't make it."

Alison strides with purpose to Michaela's side. "Guy Blanchard," she says, "I thought you were still in London."

"I just flew in this afternoon," Guy says. This is entirely obvious by his rumpled jacket and chinos. "How are you, Mrs. Freeman? That's a great dress."

"We'll all have plenty of time to catch up later," Alison says. "But right now Michaela has guests to greet. Michaela, I just saw Samuel and his new wife walk through the door. You should introduce them to Gregory. And be sure you thank them for traveling all this way." Alison turns to Guy. "Samuel is Michaela's cousin," she says. "He's a diplomat in Liberia."

Alison waves the plate of canapés away. She hasn't eaten since breakfast, though everyone is raving about the blinis. She glances around. All the guests are happily eating and drinking, chatting. It's a nice party. Alison is relieved to see that Gregory, Michaela's fiancé, has seated himself next to her own mother and is trying to make conversation. That can't be easy. The sour and disapproving look on Alison's mother's face is partly due to how hard of hearing she is, partly due to how sour and disapproving she has always been. Gregory chatters away, smiling, pointing out other people in the room. He's a good sport like that; he's always doing the right thing. He'll make a good husband for Michaela. (Gregory: Brown undergrad in History. Master's in Urban Planning from Columbia. Returned to Boston to help his uncle—the mayor's right hand man—redevelop Roxbury, the city's notorious black ghetto. Future mayor material, everybody says. A man who, at thirty, is making a name for himself.)

But where is Michaela?

Chatting with her Dartmouth friends again. Alison bites her lower lip. Should she wander over there? The bride also has her responsibilities at these things. No. Michaela hasn't neglected anyone. She can't be faulted for wanting a little break.

Just one glass of chardonnay? No.

Besides, Alison has always liked her daughter's Dartmouth friends. Whenever Alison would visit Michaela in New Hampshire, she'd make a point of taking them all out to dinner. Most of them are now lawyers—like Michaela. Or doctors, or traders on Wall Street. Alison once again debates strolling over to Michaela and the Dartmouth crowd to pick on them a little, remind them of past generosities— until she spots Guy. He is telling them a story. Everyone is laughing. Why is Guy so friendly with them? He certainly never went to Dartmouth. Then Alison remembers: Michaela and Guy were together for a long time. He was probably Michaela's date to most of their weddings. It irritates Alison that Guy infiltrates Michaela's past in the same way he is now presuming on her wedding.

Alison keeps remembering—she can't help herself. Meeting Guy for the first time. Michaela living in London, having landed a good job after Harvard Law as a patent clerk with an American firm over there. Alison and Wayne setting Michaela up in a nice two-bedroom flat in Kensington. Alison insisting on her own room for shopping trips and theater weekends, getting her own key made. Letting herself in with that key one afternoon. Discovering Michaela and Guy naked and asleep in the lounge (it's lounge in England, not living room) under a teepee erected with a broom handle and the good sheets Alison bought at Harvey Nichols. No apology from Guy upon waking. Merely covering himself with a sofa cushion and offering to make Alison a cup of tea. Michaela giggling uncontrollably. No apology from her either, until well after dinner. Dinner another ordeal. Alison taking this complete stranger and her daughter to the Savoy for Beef Wellington—making an effort. Guy refusing to touch any of it except the side vegetables. Not bothering to make something up about how he and Michaela met, which was at a private drinking club in Notting Hill, a place where the ex-pats hung out, apparently, after the pubs closed. (Guy—pronounced the French way: a trader in the London stock exchange. Successful, though only a graduate in English from some obscure school in Montreal. The son of a French Canadian dairy farmer. An accomplished pianist. A collector of classic Aston Martin Minis.)

"Doesn't Michaela look beautiful?" Alison's youngest sister Karen says in her best hostess voice. Alison hasn't noticed her sidling up.

"Yes," Alison says. Michaela is her only child.

"They're going to be a very happy couple," Karen says, placing a reassuring arm around Alison's waist.

Who is?

"Did you see Samuel and his wife?" Alison asks.

"Nobody told me she was white," Karen says.

"Me either. But she seems nice. She's French."

"Oh. Do you think it's time for my speech?" Karen asks. "People are beginning to leave."

Alison nods.

What speech?

Alison is up early the next morning. No sign of a headache, thank God. She makes herself a pot of coffee. In a few minutes she will wake Michaela. The Big Day. She and Michaela are spending most of it together: having their nails done, then their hair, then their makeup. It's an early evening wedding—six o'clock sharp at Trinity Church. Very formal. Three hundred and fifty guests. The bishop is saying the ceremony. It's costing Wayne an absolute fortune. Today he will be taking Gregory's father out to breakfast. There's a great Jewish deli right around the corner from where both families live in Brookline—very authentic. Then they will play a round of golf at Blaxton, the country club where the reception will be held. The two men are old friends. Both made *Time* magazine in the early 'seventies for moving their families to Brookline in spite of neighbourhood opposition. Both are board members of the Franklin Park Zoo. (Wayne: CEO of the largest local cable company. Boston University undergrad in business. MBA, also from BU. From one of Boston's first free black families—members of the first African American Meeting House on Beacon Hill, abolitionists alongside Frederick Douglass in the New England Anti-Slave Society; soldiers of the Union Army in the 54th Massachusetts. An excellent golfer.)

Alison pours two steaming cups of black coffee and climbs the stairs to Michaela's room. Michaela does not look beautiful this morning. She looks like hell. "How late did you stay out?" Alison asks, perching on the edge of Michaela's bed and handing her a cup. Alison tries to keep her tone light—conspiratorial. But a lot of money is riding on this day.

"I forgot how much that crowd likes to drink," Michaela says. Alison thinks smugly of the several glasses of chardonnay she did not have. "And afterward," Michaela continues, "it took ages to get a cab."

"Why didn't Gregory drive you home?" Alison asks. "Or was he drinking, too? I suppose he didn't get a proper bachelor's night out, what with the rehearsal dinner."

"He wasn't there." Michaela takes a sip of her coffee, then spits it back into the cup because it's too hot.

"Why wasn't he there?" Alison asks, later, when they're both under the heat lamps at the hairdresser.

"What are you talking about?" Michaela says, flipping the page of a dog-eared *Vogue*.

"Gregory," Alison says. She wishes she had a magazine in her lap. "Why wasn't he out with you and your friends?"

Michaela shrugs and flips another page. "Because," she says, "Gregory doesn't like my Dartmouth crowd."

"Why?"

"Because they're white and privileged and snobs," she says. She flips another couple of pages. "Because he's black and privileged and a snob."

"Was Guy there?" Alison asks, mentally flipping pages of her own magazine.

"Yes."

"I can't believe he's had the unmitigated gall to show up," Alison says, instantly regretting it.

"Why wouldn't he show up? We sent him an invitation."

Alison bites her lip. She will not get into this argument again. For some reason, Michaela refuses to understand about invitations: how invitations sent with information packets mean you're invited to come, how those sent without are merely announcements. For gifts. Michaela wanted to specify black tie, rather than leave it implicit by the time of day. Alison was only able to leave it off the invitation after showing Michaela three corroborating etiquette books.

"I'll never understand why you lived in London for so long," Alison says. They weren't talking about London. She was thinking about that teepee in the middle of the room again.

"Because I was tired of never being able to hail a cab in Boston," Michaela says. She hasn't been paying enough attention to realize Alison's non sequitur. "It's no fun standing there in the rain. The cabbies all think you're a hooker headed for some rich white guy's house in the suburbs."

This comment infuriates Alison. Michaela's father made *Time* magazine for having the courage to move his family to the suburbs during the heyday of enforced busing and race-rioting. His father before him stayed in a dying city and built up a chain of dry-cleaning stores so that his son could go to Boston University and one day move to the suburbs. Wayne went to BU so that Michaela could go to Dartmouth and Harvard. Michaela is a princess. Her tiara breaks into earrings, a brooch, and a pendant.

"Well if you liked London so much," Alison says, "why did you come home?"

"Because you made me," Michaela says. "Remember?"

It is a beautiful ceremony. Trinity Church looks beautiful, awash in white roses. Michaela makes a beautiful bride, and the bishop is resplendent in his beautiful robes. For the first time in weeks, Alison feels at peace. Nothing but a sea of tuxedoes and satin ball gowns filling up the pews. With three hundred and fifty guests, it is impossible to see Guy Blanchard or make out where he's sitting. She can relax now and enjoy her success.

Michaela swears to take Gregory as her lawfully wedded husband. She swears to honour and cherish him, in sickness and in health, so long as they both shall live. With this ring, she thee weds. They kiss. The wedding march strikes up and Alison takes Wayne's arm in the processional, behind the newlyweds, just as they have practiced. Together, they all march their way to the back of the church.

Time marching backward. Her own wedding, some thirty years ago. Immediate family only, at the Concord Baptist—the bride's family pays. A stifling church, Alison barely able to breathe beneath the simple lace veil her grandmother has tatted. Behind Alison on the right, Wayne's good Beacon Hill family in tailored, dry-cleaned suits. Grim-faced and determined. Behind her on the left, her own South End family dressed in the best they've got—but still looking threadbare and rumpled. Her side answering amen to the preacher, fluttering palmetto fans. Alison speaking her vows. Wayne mumbling his own, sweat stinging his eyes and rolling down his cheeks like tears. Alison slipping away to the bathroom to splash a little water on her face—the reception is in the church basement—finding her mother sitting on a dusty steam register by the window smoking a cigarette. What's wrong? Alison asking. A puff of smoke. Where do they get off? her mother saying; they're our own kind. Alison insisting: Wayne is a good man, the Freemans are a very good family. Another puff. I wonder about that, her mother saying, hissing smoke, stubbing out her cigarette.

I will prove you wrong. I will make you eat those words.

Michaela's receiving line is out on the church steps. It is the golden hour of the day, and the guests look wonderful milling about Copley Square. More air-kissing of in-laws. More grasping of hands, more congratulations. Alison is gratified to see that her side of the family has turned up, to the last cousin, in gowns and tuxedoes (albeit rented). She has sent the word out via her sisters: black tie only. No exceptions.

Samuel, her nephew from Liberia, steps up with his wife. They are both wearing traditional robes in sky-blue silk. Wooden necklaces of dancing gazelles and tigers and giraffes clack around their necks.

Both sport intricately knotted, batik headdresses. "Congratulations," Samuel says. "Françoise and I wish Michaela as much happiness as we have found together."

"Thank you," Alison says. "That means so much to me. Do you mind hanging back a little? We'll be doing the formal wedding photos here in Copley Square. I'd be honoured if you and Françoise would be a part of them. You've come such a long way, and you both look magnificent."

Samuel makes a slight bow and steps to the side. He and his wife put their sunglasses on, the trendy wrap-around kind favored by mountain bikers. They both light cigarettes.

A few minutes later, the Dartmouth crowd makes its way down the line. Alison, her old self now, greets them with her usual jokes. "Chip," she says, "that tux seems a little pinched across the shoulders. I'm just going to attribute it to Chelsea's good cooking." She has a nice laugh with them, accepts all of their compliments on her gown.

Guy presents his congratulations. He is wearing a charcoal gray suit, cut in a handsome three-button style, and a blood-red tie. He, however, is not handsome. Half his face is mottled by a disfiguring scar from some sort of childhood accident he refuses to talk about. Alison is triumphant. For the second time this weekend she knows for certain Michaela has made the right choice in Gregory. "Thanks for inviting me," Guy says. "It really means a lot to be included."

"The buses are over there," Alison says. "They're free. We've hired them to take the guests out to the reception."

"I know," Guy says. "Michaela told me about them last night."

Wayne's toast is too long—and he loses his way a little in the middle—but it will do. Finally, finally Alison allows wine to be poured into her glass. She gulps it down. She has another glass, and another. The reception will make the papers. It's the first African-American reception to be hosted by the Blaxton Country Club in its two hundred-year history. (Henry Blaxton or Blackstone: a hermit and a Puritan. The first white man to inhabit the Indian-infested Shawmut peninsula, later claimed by John Winthrop, Massachusetts's first governor, and renamed Boston.) All the formal photos have been taken. The bride and groom with Gregory's side. The bride and groom with Michaela's side, including Samuel and Françoise and their African costumes. The wedding party. The Dartmouth crew. The bishop. The mayor. The most important day of Alison's daughter's life has been properly documented. Alison has dispensed her duties as mother of the bride—no one could deny that. Michaela has married someone who will make a name for himself, someone who might just become mayor one day.

Out of the corner of her eye, Alison sees the glint of diamonds. Her daughter's tiara, sparkling beneath the chandeliers. Michaela is standing at the edge of the parquet dance floor, talking to Guy. Their heads are a little too close together. Alison watches Michaela place a hand on Guy's shoulder. That does it! She lurches up, knocking over her wine glass. She careens to the rescue of her wicked, wicked daughter. She says, "Guy, I can't believe you have the nerve to show up at a black-tie wedding in a suit." She has meant this to sound like a joke—like her comment to Chip earlier about his ill-fitting tux.

"Mother!" Michaela gasps.

"I'm sorry, Mrs. Freeman," Guy says. "It didn't say anything about it on the invitation." He is not upset. He has no idea what she's talking about. He's just being his usual, polite self. Refusing to challenge her openly, sneaking around behind her back.

"Everybody knows an evening wedding is black tie," Alison says. Why can't she stop herself? "Didn't your parents teach you anything?" Alison's ear's are ringing. It's as if the three of them have suddenly been enveloped by a bubble of silence. Everything around Alison— the dance floor, the littered tables, the milling guests—everything shimmers and vibrates on the other side of an invisible soapy membrane. She can see her life carrying on, out there. But her future, her future is being told right now, on the inside of this imaginary crystal ball. (Alison: who, exactly, is Alison?)

"My parents are dairy farmers in Quebec," Guy says. His voice is as quiet as a prayer, as calm as the whir of a palmetto fan. "If you want me to turn up in a tuxedo, Mrs. Freeman, you kind of have to tell me."

The clamour of drunken guests. The clank of china and crystal.

The wheeze of an accordion sawing its way through *Fiddler on the Roof.*

"She didn't mean it," Michaela says to Guy. "She doesn't really care. It was just a joke." Then Michaela turns to Alison. The plea in her eyes is simple. Tell him, it says. Please tell him. "We're so glad you could make it, aren't we?"

Alison excuses herself. She makes for the women's room, her vision reduced to a tiny tunnel of purpose—air. Once there, she locks herself into the corner stall. She won't have very long before Michaela comes chasing after her, before Michaela demands to know what her problem is.

She sits motionless, waiting for the migraine.

The Almond Eater

Since moving to London, he has begun to eat three almonds a day. He takes them in the morning with a mug of peppermint tea. He places three nuts in a row, along the window sill over his kitchen sink. One by one he pops them into his mouth, chewing each thoroughly, washing each away with a sip of peppermint tea.

On Saturdays he buys them by the quarter pound at the Portobello Market. There is an herbalist there who sells them in a makeshift stall. She sits at a flimsy card table at the food end of things below Elgin Crescent. The herbalist is Irish, a woman with fiery hair that zigzags out of her scalp like lightning bolts. She has topaz eyes. Almonds, she has whispered more than once, are an Atlantean panacea long since forgotten about. If he eats three of them a day he will not be bothered by health problems for as long as he lives.

On Sunday afternoons he blanches the entire quarter pound in boiling water. When the nuts are cool, he can slip their outer husks off as easily as he imagines a silk blouse slipping off the shoulders of his fiery herbalist. He wonders, as he shucks them at his sink, how she has come to know about these long-lost Atlantean cures. Into his mouth he pops the first almond of his day, the first of his week. (Where he's from, they count Sunday as the first day, not the last.) He eats the second almond, then the third. And just where, he wonders, are the Atlanteans now?

***

Since moving to London, he has begun acupuncture once a fortnight. Radha Bindi is his therapist. She is treating him for general wellness. Once a fortnight he enters a tiny white cubicle at the Zen Centre, a quaint mews house behind Waterloo Station. He removes his shoes and watch, loosens his belt, lies on the crisp white paper covering the examination table. There is a mobile hanging above his head—origami swans meant to distract him from the needles. Swans swimming gently among the stars he will no doubt see while he is being stuck.

Eventually Radha arrives to take his pulses. She examines his tongue, sniffs the back of his neck and chest. She questions him about his dreams and bowel movements and food cravings. She counts out the vertebrae of his back, making notations on his skin with a blue ball-point pen. She inserts needles into her ink diagrams and goes away. When she comes back, she removes the needles. Then, depending on the yin and the yang of his various organs, she might burn mugwort root on points at his elbows and wrists or manipulate needles in carefully chosen points at his armpits, stomach, and palms.

Sometimes he feels nothing, nothing at all. But sometimes, while Radha is manipulating her needles, he feels thousands of volts of electricity coursing through his body. He can actually hear the crackle of something being rechanneled, realigned. At times like these it feels as though Radha has touched off a blowtorch with her needles. He imagines dozens of tiny blue flames hissing from the pin-prick leaks in his skin. But when he looks, he sees nothing but blue ball-point ink marks.

Twice now Radha has waved her hand over his stomach, frowning. "Tell me," she has said on both occasions, "when was the last time you had a thorough check-up by your doctor?"

Since moving to London, he has not telephoned his work colleagues or friends or family to let them know where he his. He has not left a forwarding address for credit card bills or birthday cards, has not put his loft on the market. For all anyone knows, he is still right there. Maybe a little hard to reach in recent months. Busy.

He has entered the United Kingdom on a tourist visa though he has no plans to leave. He did not pack any of his expensive prescriptions. In fact, he flushed them all down the toilet two hours before his flight. He would not risk being turned away.

For as long as he lives in London he will not need an English bank account. He can use his ATM card at any Barclays branch. He will not need a job. It will take months to charge his credit cards up to the limit. He will not have his cutlery and vacuum cleaner and bed linen shipped from home. The flat he took in Notting Hill, like most of those he considered, came completely furnished. Getting it was easy enough. Estate agents never bother to check overseas references for flats above a certain price range.

What he has learned from all of this: that packing for a week is the same as packing for ever; if you have enough underwear and socks for seven days—a deck of playing cards—you can continue on indefinitely. His family and friends will, sooner or later, have to get used to the idea of his absence.

Since moving to London, he has begun to spend his days in the Notting Hill library, reading about the lost civilization of Atlantis. He has just finished a lengthy, incomplete dialogue by Plato. Atlantis, according to Plato, was an island as large as a continent, beyond the pillars of Hercules. Once a peace treaty was reached, the Greeks and their gods began to travel there frequently, on holiday. His reading includes a biography of an American prophet, Edgar Cayce. In a series of trances Cayce claimed Atlantis to be the mother pyramid culture of the Egyptians, Mesopotamians, and Aztecs. The great flood of biblical times, according to Cayce, resulted from the sinking of the Atlantean continent. So Noah was Atlantean, as was Ra, as was Quetzal-coatyl. He has also glanced at other, more speculative sources which suggest that Atlantis might have been a settlement from outer space. One author tries to link disappearances in the Bermuda Triangle with abandoned Atlantean laser beams, long since sunken to the bottom of the Caribbean by earthquakes. A truth has begun to emerge: that human beings have a need to blame cataclysmic disasters for the random and ordinary misfortunes that befall them— and that they admire the past to excess.

***

Since moving to London, he has taken to setting his alarm for two o'clock Sunday morning so that he can be out dancing by three. (He still considers this to be a Saturday evening activity, like other Londoners.) There is a nightclub he likes, in an abandoned part of the Charing Cross Tube station. Only men go there, men on mood elevating drugs. He takes these as well, just before leaving the flat. He needs no prescription. He simply buys them in the toilet of the club with cash he has drawn out of a Barclays machine. On an early Sunday morning, he'll set three bluish tablets on the sill of his kitchen window and swallow them one by one.

In the tunnel he dances in complete darkness, alone, with hundreds and hundreds of damp, slippery men. All he can see is their eyes which blaze. The music is so loud he cannot hear it. This suits him. Dancing is not seeing in that abandoned Tube tunnel at Charing Cross; it is not hearing. It is merely movement in time to the rattle of his own bones, flotation on the neap tides of chemical ebb and flow.

Dancing, his thoughts turn to the herbalist's topaz eyes, to Radha Bindi's insistent fingers, to the sweetness of his mother's full breast, to a woman with a man's name who will never bear his child. All this in the few moments before his thoughts skitter away and slide off the edge into the abyss.

At about ten or eleven o'clock in the morning he takes one of the slippery damp men home. Neither of them speaks during the unlicensed cab ride. They both stare out opposing windows at entirely different Sunday afternoons. Neither do they speak in the flat, even as they undress each other, clean each other like cats with their tongues. They don't in fact utter a single word until, in the heat of embrace, the blazing-eyed man pants: "There's something important I have to tell you before this goes any farther."

Until he replies, "I know; that's why I've chosen you."

Almonds—particularly the bitter ones—contain traces of cyanide. He has read they can be quite lethal, when eaten in large enough quantities.

Loss of Gravity

1. THE IDES OF MARC

I'm Simone. Twenty-nine years old, a decent enough graphic designer and mother of a three-year-old named Phoebe. Everyone thinks I'm much too young to have lost my husband Marc. Well, I am. Marc was broadsided in his vintage Beetle by a drunken SUV driver on the Jacques-Cartier Bridge on March 15—six months ago this weekend. I don't even have the luxury of wishing the other driver dead. Everyone thinks I look like hell, but they're always telling me how good I look. I look like hell, trust me. And I hope it goes without saying: I wish I were dead too.

Last week I got a warning at work. My boss assured me he understood what I was going through—everyone is always saying that too—but there were growing concerns about my ability to give one hundred per cent to the team. (This from the man who disappears for whole chunks of the day because he's cheating on his wife during business hours.) I reminded him I had a week of vacation coming, plus two weeks of comp time left over from our busy season. Maybe I should take a short leave of absence, I said, to get my head together. He agreed—what choice did he have?—but he's probably interviewing for my replacement.

So anyway, here I am, at my mother-in-law's beach house on Cape Cod. Day one: getting my head together, getting over Marc. I've brought a three-week supply of Dorothy Sayers mysteries, a full prescription of anti-depressants, and my watercolours. I'm leaving Phoebe with Phyllis, the mother-in-law, in Montreal.

I'm not getting over anything. I'm getting drunk.

Phyllis drove me all the way down here, to settle me in. We left Montreal well before dawn, dropping Phoebe off with some woman from Phyllis's bridge club. Hours went by—lots of trees—and then suddenly we were crossing the bridge onto the Cape. Phyllis immediately pulled into the nearest supermarket to cram the trunk full of groceries. You should have seen her at that Stop-N-Shop, racing up and down the aisles, throwing toilet paper and peppermint tea into the shopping cart; bubble bath and sandwich meat, tanning lotion and fresh peaches. I just loped along behind. (Here's what I put in that shopping cart, my contributions to my salvation: a case of Labatts Blue—Marc's brand—and an embarrassingly large bottle of cheap Cabernet. Screw top. Screw it.) Phyllis paid for everything. Then she put it all away when we got to her house in Truro, which is basically the fuck-you finger of Massachusetts. She made up my bed, took all the slip covers off the living room furniture, did a little dusting. In less than an hour, she was boarding her flight home. (She's leaving me with her car. I haven't gotten around to replacing the crushed Beetle yet.)

Phyllis sent out all her thank-you-for-the-flowers notes like a week after Marc's funeral. (She lost her second husband to melanoma a few years back, so she's had some practice.) I haven't sent out any thank-you's yet. I think you get up to a year. Or am I confusing that with weddings?

2. INDEPENDENT DINING

Night is falling and I haven't eaten a single peach. But I am on my second six-pack. I've spent the afternoon staring out across the harbour. I've made friends with a wooden rocking chair on the screen porch. The green paint is chipping off its arms. I'm whale-watching, helping the chipping process along. I'm only getting up to pee. I haven't seen a single whale yet. But I'm not that worried, I've got three weeks. Imagine: three whole weeks of this. The phone rings; it's Phyllis, of course. She's back in Montreal—(already?)—just checking in with me. Would I like to speak with Phoebe before she puts her to bed?

Hi baby, Mommy misses you. No, darling; I'm not with Daddy. I'll explain it all when I get back, okay? Be a good girl, okay? Now put Granny back on the phone.

I climb into Phyllis's car. I peel out of the driveway in a satisfying spray of clamshells. At the end of her road I turn left onto Route 6. I can never remember if that's Up Cape or Down.

Yes, I'm driving drunk. I admit it: I can't face that obscenely full refrigerator. My plan is to eat at the first place with more than three cars in the parking lot. But everything's boarded up for the season, and I'm frankly running out of Cape. I'm just cresting Pilgrim Heights. What's left of Massachusetts curls out before me. Maybe it's more of a trigger finger than the bird. Off to my right is the murky outline of the Provincetown Monument. It commemorates the landing of the Mayflower even though it's actually a bad copy of a bell tower in Siena. Perfect. I hit the gas.

In P-Town I end up at this hopelessly romantic guesthouse with a restaurant attached to it. Ten minutes till the kitchen closes. The waiter is not happy to see me. Table for the independent diner this evening? He seats me near the fireplace, which is too hot. I order a Stoli martini with extra olives. Olives, that's what Phyllis should have bought at Stop-N-Shop. Or those little cocktail onions. She could easily have skipped the twelve-pack of quilted toilet paper.

The older couple next to me has just asked for the check. Across the way, a sad-looking man sips coffee and reads a guide book in German. The waiter brings my martini and suggests I order right away—the kitchen. Never mind, I tell him, I don't feel like dining independently after all; how much do I owe him? A slightly awkward moment. He apologizes. He doesn't mean to rush me, it's really no trouble. It's just that the staff are all going out tonight. There's a bonfire at Herring Cove Beach. But it'll keep till they get there. What would I like?

I burst into tears. Uh-oh. The alcohol, I guess. Phyllis's fucking emotional efficiency. My boss. The vagrant wish for a pressing, after-dinner engagement.

The couple next to me arch their eyebrows and scrape their chairs back. Time to go! The German signals for his check. The waiter—a study in dismay—tells me he'll be right back. Just what he needs: crazy crying woman at closing time. He bids the old geezers goodnight, attends to the German who wants to pay in cash. I blow my nose on the cloth napkin in my lap—it's an emergency—and take a good slug of my martini. Then another. The waiter escorts the German to the door and flips the Open sign to Closed.

I close my eyes and wonder, not for the first time, whose brilliant idea this was to shuffle me off to the Cape. I'm pretty sure it wasn't mine. I had sort of planned on sitting around my apartment in my sweatpants for three weeks, eating Ben & Jerry's out of the container until I exploded. Simone's always loved her watercolours. What she needs is to get back into her painting. It'll take her mind off things. As if I don't already spend enough time alone. I'm waiting, waiting for the sound of my check to be slapped in front of me. Silence. I open my eyes. The waiter is at the bar, pouring himself a Jack Daniels. He wanders over and takes a seat.

—I'm Michael.

—Simone. Sorry about that.

—Bad day?

—My first time alone in a restaurant, Michael. Some jerk killed my husband a couple of months ago in a car crash. This is how well I'm dealing with it.

—We're just about to have our dinner in the kitchen. Grab your drink. You can eat with us.

This, Simone, is the where you should scrape together what's left of your dignity. This is where you should thank him for his random act of kindness, pay him for the drink, leave him a big tip. This is where you should get yourself a cup of strong black coffee and drink every drop of it in the 7-Eleven parking lot before creeping back to Truro. But you can't. Because this is how well you're dealing with it. So you grab your martini and you follow Michael into the kitchen.

Michael lies to the others with facility. Girls! Listen up, he says, this is my friend Simone. She just got into town, like, five minutes ago and her cupboards are bare. We're taking pity on her. He turns to me, then. Simone, the one in chef's drag is Gabriel. And the white trash over at the sink is Peter. But you can just ignore him, he's the help. The busboy, Peter, brings an extra plate and some cutlery. He plops himself down next to me. It's his last night in this godforsaken hell-hole, he tells me. If I need anything else, I'm just going to have to get it myself. Nobody knows the soap suds he's seen. His career as a hand model is ruined.

The chef, Gabriel, sets a large bowl of mixed greens in the center of the table. He begins tossing them with balsamic vinegar, olive oil, and a little dry mustard. He's an astonishing-looking man in his mid-thirties: green eyes the colour of Chinese silk, closely cropped salt-and-pepper hair, a swimmer's body under those chef whites. Why don't straight men ever look like this?

Michael, my long-lost college friend, sets four wine goblets on the table and splashes a little Pinot Grigio into Gabriel's glass. Gabriel tastes it and nods, Michael seats himself on my other side and pours the bottle out. Gabriel raises his goblet, and we all follow suit. He thanks Michael and Peter for a wonderful summer; he hopes they'll return next May. He welcomes me to P-Town. Ching-ching. *Bon appétit.*

I'm starving. I realize this as soon as I've had my first bite of salad. I've been skipping a lot of meals lately. Not much of an independent diner, I'm afraid. A meal, by my definition, requires at least two willing participants. (Sorry, three-year-olds don't count.) In fact, I can't think of anything more ill-advised than the elaborate preparation and consumption of food by just one person. Not when there's Oreos. I help myself to more salad, though this is in clear breach of the guest-host relationship. I haven't spoken a word yet. A meal requires conversation from each of its participants. I should at least tell Gabriel the food's good.

Screw it, Simone. These men are used to strangers turning up at mealtime. It's their lifestyle. They'd much rather gossip about tonight's customers: the unruly lesbian birthday party, the regulars, the anniversary couples, that weird German guy. When Peter asks again how you know Michael, just remind him "college". He'll gather up your salad plate and forget the answer like before. When Gabriel asks you what brings you to the Cape so late in the season, tell him it's your favourite time of year. He'll just nod and open a nice little Napa Valley Merlot.

For our main, we're having what's left of tonight's special: roasted duck in a blueberry sauce. The birthday lesbian didn't like it and sent it back. I'm not crazy about it either, but I find myself cleaning my plate. Conversation veers to the evening ahead. Turns out, it's not just any bonfire. It's the End-of-the-Season-Townies-Only bonfire with special drag appearances. Turns out, Peter is one of these: Princess Panoply from the Planet Love. Clever, I say. Lost on the gay boys, Peter sighs. Philistines in tight white Calvin Klein underwear. They're always getting it wrong and calling him Penelope. I try to imagine Peter in drag. I just can't see it. He's young and athletic-looking and hip. Gorgeous teeth.

—Why don't you come along, Simone? It should be a trip.
—But it's "townies only" you said.
—Honey, you're eating in the kitchen. Let's not split hairs.
—Fangs in, Penelope. She didn't mean it like that.
—I'm just dishin' her cause I like her accent. I, Princess Panoply, dub thee, Simone, honorary townie with all the honours and privileges of same. What's for dessert?
—I should be getting home. I've already imposed enough on your hospitality.
—Sit yourself back down. You're coming with us; it's all settled. Who knows, you might meet the girl of your dreams.
—She's not a dyke, Pot-O-Pee.
—Honey, they all look like dykes to me.

We decide to skip dessert; we're watching our figures. Instead, Gabriel cuts up a few mackintosh apples while Michael makes us cappuccinos and laces them with Kaluà. Meanwhile, Peter and I rinse plates and put them in the dishwasher. He tells me he and Gabe are having an affair. He swears me to secrecy; Michael doesn't know this. Gabe owns a house in Wellfleet with his boyfriend of eleven years. Boyfriend is away this week, visiting his parents in New Jersey. Tonight will be their last together. Tomorrow, Gabe will escort Peter to the Greyhound station in Hyannis; Peter is starting the graduate architecture program at Harvard this fall. But first, they will be spending the day on Nantucket, just the two of them. Peter has never been on a real island before.

Michael wants to know what we're whispering about. Girl talk, Peter says, don't be jealous. Michael says he is jealous; after all, he hasn't seen me since college. Good, Peter says, then he won't mind taking me up to their room in the attic to lend me a pretty sweater, just like in college. It's going to get chilly out on the beach.

I start to laugh. I can't help it. My day-to-day life is never this weird. Usually I wake up, drop my daughter off at daycare, design mutual fund prospectuses for eight hours, and pick her up again on my way home. I make Phoebe's supper, I skip mine. I watch a little TV, then go to bed having no idea what I've just watched. Sometimes I sleep, sometimes I don't. Today, though. Today I woke up and moved to the Cape. I drank a six-pack of Labatts and whale-watched. I drove drunk to a restaurant fifteen miles away. I burst into tears in front of the waiter and he invited me to dinner. Now I'm going to a party on the beach. Provincetown. I've never been this far out there before.

4. Bonfire of the Vanities

We all pile into Gabe's 1967 Cadillac convertible. Tomato red, of course. The top's down, but it kind of has to be. Princess Panoply's wig. It's sort of a Marie-Antoinette number made out of Christmas tree tinsel. The rest of Peter's outfit makes him look like a majorette from outer-space. I don't tell him this. I'm not sure it'll come off as a compliment. He takes the front seat, out of the wind. In the back, I advise Michael to tell me the name of his college. He shrugs. He says he's never quite made it to college. I choose Villanova for us. I don't have a clue which state Villanova's in, but I've always liked the sound of that name.

The party is in full swing by the time we pull into the Herring Cove parking lot. A drag policewoman brandishing a flashlight greets us at the edge of the sand. We all know the rules, she says: no alcohol on the beach, no controlled substances, no public nudity, no defacement of public property. Does anyone want to buy pot? Michael asks for a couple of joints, pays her, and leads us over the dune. We head for the orange glow.

The bonfire itself is enormous. Its nucleus looks suspiciously like a picnic table. We're careful to spread our blanket upwind. Michael uncorks another bottle of Merlot. Princess Panoply entrusts me with her automatic focus camera and dashes off to join the backup chorus of a drag duet lip-synching "Enough Is Enough". Gabriel offers to make us some s'mores. So it's just me and Michael. I always dreamed I'd find the perfect lover. I look up. The sky is drenched in stars. Michael encourages me to lean into him. He wraps his arms around me. We both look up. He tells me I shouldn't be surprised if Gabe and Peter disappear off into the dunes. They're having a secret affair. He swears me to secrecy; they don't know that he knows.

—There's something else I should tell you, Simone.

—Oh for heaven's sake, Michael. I know you're gay. You're safe with me.

—Give me break. Listen, I lost my lover last winter. After twelve years together. So I kind of understand what you're going through.

No more tears. Enough is enough.

—Did he suffer, Michael?

—We both did. And it isn't over. It was his house and his money. The family challenged the legality of the will and they won. They threw me out. That's why I'm waiting tables down here; Gabe's an old friend.

—Are you okay?

—Do you mean have I got it?

—No, actually. I mean are you, you know, okay?

The drag queens end their number and begin a new one. It's something from the 'thirties or 'forties. I don't know it. I flash back to

Marc's funeral: to my parents, trying to muster grief when all they can manage is relief that it was Marc and not me. To Phyllis, too wrapped up in the actual event—the music, the pall bearers, the speakers, the buffet luncheon, the flowers—to feel much of anything. And there's me, standing there, holding my daughter on my hip, trying to explain to her what's going on, failing miserably at grief because all I can feel is rage. A mind-numbing, all-consuming hatred. For Marc, for leaving me in the lurch. Again.

I turn around and face Michael directly. Thinning blond hair, little round glasses. Ordinary nose, a completely ordinary-looking guy. It's not fair, I tell him, what his lover's family has done to him. It's bigoted and cold-hearted and inhuman. He agrees. But his therapist has finally given him some decent advice for a change. It's better to keep things separate: the laws governing marriage versus the laws of love.

The loss of love.

I wipe my eyes on the sleeve of his sweatshirt, thankful, for once, for the misunderstanding, *faute d'accent*.

It's Gloria Gaynor next. A general roar of approval. People are jumping up all over the place to dance. I grab Michael's hand and haul him to his feet. Princess Panoply and Gabriel join in. We hug each other and spin, the sand squeaking beneath our feet. Peter is insisting all four of us fly to Nantucket tomorrow morning—someplace I've actually been. It'll only cost forty dollars each, he says. We'll go shopping, have a little lunch, rent mopeds. We can take the ferry back to Hyannis. Gabriel jams a white chocolate s'more into his face. We all take bites out of it while we spin. I imagine us with wings, taking flight, spiraling up into the stars. Laws of nature. Laws of the universe. But the sensation is more like falling. We're definitely going to fall. Laws of gravity. We end up in a big messy, tinselly, sticky heap. We're fine, though. We will survive.

5. The Secret Garden

It's only a matter of time before the real police raid the party. Panic ensues when somebody notices the blue flashing lights over the dune. Bottles are dumped out, nickel bags are buried in the sand. Michael and I part company with Gabe and Peter in the mayhem. They've got the bedspread with them; they're seeking refuge in the dunes. Peter makes us swear, though, that we'll be on the front porch of the guesthouse at eight-thirty sharp. Our plane is at ten-thirty. We watch them slink off together, Peter with cha-cha heels in hand, wig listing badly to starboard; Gabe still gorgeous, even from behind, even in the dark.

Michael and I take our chances in the general exodus back to town. We don't have our thumbs out for very long before a pickup truck stops. We climb into the back with Josie and the Pussycats. Everyone is going on to the A House, the only dance bar still open, for last call. We decline. Soon, we are alone on Commercial Street. The fog is rolling in; everything is going watercoloury and soft: edges all feathery, light with too much water in it. Michael suddenly remembers the two joints in his breast pocket. We each light one and begin walking.

Flash back to the Ides of Marc. Dinner is on the table. So where the fuck is he? I don't dare call his office, anymore. It freaks me out when the receptionist tells me he left at six. I don't know what's worse: eating alone when he doesn't show up, or eating alone when he's sitting across the table from me. The phone rings and I jump. Don't get your hopes up, I tell myself, it's probably just Phyllis. It isn't Phyllis.

Hug me, I tell Michael. He stops walking and hugs me.

We're in front of a beautiful Victorian guesthouse with walkways planted in a riot of red geraniums. They're everywhere, ferocious, defiant. He bends down and starts pulling up two of the plants by their roots. Don't just stand there, he whispers, dig! I manage to dislodge two of my own from the moist, salty ground. There's a guesthouse farther along Commercial Street, Michael tells me, one that doesn't have a single plant in front of it, just a fence with half the pickets missing. When we get to it a moment later, we dig four evenly spaced holes along the fence. I hum "Enough Is Enough" while we transplant our geraniums where they will be better appreciated.

Back at Michael's guesthouse. He insists I stay over—it would be crazy for me to drive home at this hour. He takes a key from a hook behind the desk and we go to Room 6, Route 6, lucky six. Six months later. We get undressed and climb into bed. Again I realize

I'm starving. But I relax into it. I recognize this skin hunger for what it is. I snuggle my shoulder blades into Michael's chest. He buries his nose in the nape of my neck. Soon he is sleeping, soon I am on Nantucket.

6. WHALE WATCHING

The four of us are driving to Hyannis in Gabe's Cadillac. We're playing the AM radio full-blast. Gabe and Peter are in the front seat, holding hands. Michael and I are snuggled low in the back. We're running late. It's ten-twenty by the time we pull into the airport parking lot. We race up to the ticket counter, breathless. There are exactly four seats left. Gabe throws it all on his credit card. We'll sort the money thing out at the end of the day, on the ferry back.

What we weigh matters. I'm instructed to sit next to the pilot since I'm the lightest. Gabe and Michael are told to take the next two seats. Peter, to his horror, has to sit with a nun. Two more nuns bring up the rear. Pretty unlikely we'll crash today, the pilot whispers to me, firing up the engines. We fly right through any puffy white clouds in our path. We jump into a taxi at Nantucket airport. It's driven by a little old lady. She takes us to the cobbled center of town. She's completely deaf. The ride costs five dollars.

We cut a deal with the owner of the moped rental place: we'll only pay twenty-five dollars each, half his regular rate. He doesn't care; he's made his money for the year. After our safety lesson, we head for the opposite end of the island, racing each other, attempting Shriner formations. Along the way we pass lighthouses and cornfields, weather-beaten old cottages. We wish we lived here. We hope this day will never end. Enormous sunflowers bow down to us as we careen by.

In Siasconset we stop at the package store and buy a gallon jug of screw-top Cabernet. We drive our mopeds right onto the beach. We take all sorts of photos of each other with Peter's camera because we've forgotten to take any at the bonfire: Peter and Gabe, Michael and I, all four of us together, each of us alone. We lie in a heap and whale watch. Michael thinks he sees one, but he doesn't really. It's just the crest of an unusually large wave.

We return to Nantucket village with barely enough time to board the ferry. We've sprung for first-class—it only costs five dollars more—and there's a full bar with a free platter of sweaty cheese cubes. We order wine and gobble half the platter. Old ladies and men look on, sternly. We've been behaving badly for almost twenty-four hours. Why in hell should we stop now?

Stop now, Simone.

You're not going to Nantucket tomorrow. You're going to let Gabriel have his private day with Peter. But you know exactly how it will go: the plane, the nuns, the taxi, the mopeds, the sunflowers, the beach. You can imagine every single detail of it because you've been to Nantucket before. You honeymooned there with Marc. It was Marc who thought he saw a whale at Siasconset beach.

Let Gabe and Peter stand alone at the bow of the ferry as it pulls into Hyannis harbour. Allow them a passionate good-bye kiss. Gabe is going to have to get into his Cadillac and drive home to Wellfleet alone. Peter is going to have to take that long bus ride up to Boston. Gabe's lover is on his way back from New Jersey, Peter has school to think about now. They will never see each other again.

And you, Simone. Tomorrow you are going to drive back to Truro with an enormous hangover. You're packing everything back up into the trunk of your car—the peaches and sandwich meat, your watercolours and paperback mysteries—and you're driving straight home to Montreal to rescue your daughter from the evil clutches of Phyllis. You'll open a can of Spaghetti-Os, something you both can eat in front of the TV. No sweetie, your daddy loved you very much but he's not coming home. He can't. Ever. It's just you and me now, okay?

But tonight, Simone, tonight you're going to lie here in Michael's arms. And the two of you are going to sleep the sleep of the dead.

Last Chance Texaco

I woke up this morning.

It was in a bed I'd never slept in, in a town I'd never been to. I found myself naked under a quilt sewn by a stranger. It occurred to me that this might be heaven, this tiny white room with a big bed and gauzy white curtains. But I soon gave up on that idea. Why would I ever expect to find myself there?

"Morning," she said.

"Good morning," I answered. "I didn't see you."

"Been here all night." She was sitting on the only other piece of furniture in the room, an over-stuffed blue chair. She was wearing a fuzzy blue bathrobe. A blue lady on a blue cloud.

"I made a mess," I said.

"You certainly did," she giggled. It wasn't funny.

"I guess I'm alive."

"You got that right," she said.

She told me her name was Amanda. She would fix me an egg if I wanted. But then I'd have to be on my way. I asked her where my suit was. She told me all but the pants had to be thrown out because of the blood. I could borrow a pair of Avery's jeans for now. I asked who Avery was. She told me he was the guy who towed my car in last night. Then I remembered him. Nice smile.

"How is my car?"

"Dead. Dead as you almost were," she said.

"Sorry about that," I said.

"Are you some kind of nut?"

"I don't think so," I told her.

"Dangerous?"

"No," I lied, "just a loser."

She considered this. "I didn't find a wallet on you. What's your name?"

"Alex." Another lie.

"So how do you want your eggs, Alex?"

"Scrambled," I said and we smiled.

"There's a bathrobe on the back of the door. I think you're probably strong enough to get up and eat in the kitchen."

"I'll be fine," I said.

She squinted at me, then left the room.

So now my name is Alex. I'll decide on a last name when I need one. I know exactly where my wallet is; it's under the driver's seat of my car with my cell phone. That's where I always stow them—to save my back—when I'm driving any sort of distance.

I woke up this morning in tiny, light-filled room with no identity. It's giving me the first real appetite I've had in months.

Last night I was on my way to the Mexican border when my Mercedes broke down in the Middle of Nowhere, Texas. The engine went dead—I don't know why. It could have been any one of a thousand things that go wrong with a car when you don't take care of it. As I coasted to the side of the road, the last of my big plans came to a halt. I just sat there in the unbearable heat of Texas summer; hood up, head down, door open, legs dangling in the dust. Surrounding me, as far as I could see into the twilight, were miles of oil fields. Gray horizon heaving like an ocean. Gas jets burning off like dragons hissing against the darkness.

An hour went by. No cars. Calm evaporating off my skin. I tried the radio a couple of times to see if I could catch the news, forgetting each time that it was dead, too. No bars on the cell phone, no cell service since Gonzales. I found myself wishing for things: a cool shower, a fresh shirt, two days of uninterrupted sleep. I wanted for today not to have happened, for someone else to please drive down this pot-holed little road. I wanted to throw up, but couldn't. I hadn't eaten anything since Dallas.

Another hour went by. Finally I saw headlights coming toward me. I resisted opening the glove compartment to peek at the revolver hidden under the owner's manual.

"Howdy," he said. He was a handsome man with shiny dark hair in a ponytail. American Indian, I think, or maybe Italian. He had a baby blue pickup. An old one, with a big red dog in the back.

"It just died on me. I'm not much with cars," I said.

"Will she turn over at all?"

"At first, but not now. Even the radio's dead."

"Like me to take a look?" he asked.

"Do you know about cars?"

"Hope so," he said, smiling. "I got a Texaco station about six or eight miles up the road."

"Then by all means," I said.

He got out of his pickup, grabbing a toolbox from the back. He shone a flashlight on the engine. "Looks like the crankshaft's fried," he said. "It won't do any good to jump her. I could go get my tow truck and bring her back to the Texaco. There's more light there."

"Can you fix it?" I asked.

"Don't know. You may have seized her up. I won't be able to tell for sure till I can see what I'm doing."

"I don't have a lot money on me. How much for the tow?"

"Tow's free," he said. "I'm not going to leave you out here for the coyotes."

I opened the passenger door of his pickup. That's when the dog in the back started barking.

"Hush, Blue," he said, hopping behind the wheel. "Funny," he said, "He usually only barks at Gypsies and Mexicans."

"When was the last time you put oil in her?" he asked. It was late. We'd hauled my car back to the station.

"Why?" I said. "Does it need a can of oil? Let's put some in."

"Mister, it's a little late for that. You've burnt her up."

"What does that mean?" I said.

"It means you have to replace just about the whole engine, which isn't going to be cheap. If you want, I can try and buy a secondhand one off a scrap guy I know in Gonzales. But I wouldn't get your hopes up. If it ain't a Ford, there ain't much call for it around here."

"Are you sure it's dead? I mean, we can't just fix it to get me a little farther?"

"Deader than a bastard," he said, "Where you headed?"

I asked him if I could use his restroom. He shrugged and told me I'd find the key on a hook inside the office door. I got my shaving kit out of the back seat and said excuse me. I locked myself inside and turned the water on. The sink plug didn't work. First I sat on the toilet seat, my head in my hands, reciting every filthy word I could remember. Then I pulled myself together. I knelt in front of the toilet bowl. I broke the blade out of my shaver and made two long gashes in each wrist, trying to follow the largest, bluest veins. I crooked my arms and sank them into the bowl. The water was cold; it felt good on my skin. Before long it turned bright red. A few minutes went by—bright red minutes. I couldn't tell if the noise was that Indian pounding on the door, or just the bright red blood pounding in my temples before draining out of my wrists into the toilet.

A little boy stares at me from across the kitchen table. His spoon is poised in mid-air while a pile of scrambled eggs sits cold on his plate. Blink, I want to say, please blink. "What's your name?" I ask, offering a smile. He stares into my eyes.

"His name is Brit," Amanda says, bringing me more coffee. "Say howdy to Mr. Alex, Brit." Brit just stares.

"That's an interesting name," I say to him.

"It's short for Great Britain," Amanda says from over by the stove, "Where his daddy's from, and where he no doubt returned after knocking me up."

"How long you staying?" Brit finally says, his spoon swooping into the eggs.

"Mr. Alex is leaving right after breakfast," Amanda says.

"You sick?" he asks me.

"A little," I tell him.

"Your car's deader than a bastard, Avery says."

"Watch the cussing, Brit." Amanda returns to the table with the coffee pot. My cup is still full from her last trip. She wanders back to the stove.

"But Avery said—"

"Everything Avery says ain't for company."

"Why are your arms all wrapped up?" Brit asks me, pointing at my wrists with his spoon.

"I had a little accident last night," I say, winking. "But I'm fine now. Want to race to see who can finish their eggs first?"

"Deal," he says, beginning to eat with purpose.

I continue to sit at the kitchen table after Amanda has cleared our plates, long after Brit has gone outside to play. The only thing between me and a very uncertain future is this half-empty coffee cup.

"Where were you headed?" Amanda asks, taking Brit's chair. She has her own cup of coffee.

"South," I say. "I'm out of work. Thought I'd stay with a cousin in Brownsville and start looking for a job."

"Can't you call him to come and get you?"

"No," I say. I can't think of a reasonable lie why not, so I sip cold coffee instead.

"How about your wife?" she asks. She's looking at my wedding ring. I've forgotten to take it off.

"Divorced," I say.

"Look," she says, after a pause. "No wallet, no job. You make a mess of my bathroom and then you won't call anyone to come and get you? Can you think of any reason why I shouldn't call my cousin Jasper, the sheriff?"

"No," I say. Suddenly I feel tired. Narcoleptic. "Please," I say, and I can hear the torn edge in my own voice, "please just let me sit here for a while longer. Then do whatever you have to do. But it's nice here. I just want to finish my coffee, okay?"

Amanda sizes me up from across the rim of her own cup. "You're in trouble. I can smell it on you like last night's liquor. You going to tell me why you're on the run?"

I listen to the hum of the refrigerator. Nothing comes to me. I resort to the truth. "I thought if I could drive fast enough, I'd out-distance a life full of problems. But when my car broke down, I had plenty of time—out there in the desert—to realize my biggest problem was sitting right there in the getaway car."

Amanda snorts. "You been watching too much TV," she says.

"So what are you going to do?" I ask.

"Wait for Avery to come in for lunch."

"Where is he?"

"Out pumping gas."

"You're not from Texas, are you," Avery says, seating himself at the table. I'm still in the flannel robe Amanda gave me. I haven't moved all morning, except once to take a leak. I feel a little shaky, dizzy, but I'm fine. I guess I hadn't bled nearly enough before Avery knocked the restroom door in last night.

"Got one hell of a New York accent," Amanda says from over by the stove.

"New York's right," I say.

"Car's got Texas plates, though," Avery says. He pours himself a tall glass of milk.

"Bought it in Dallas," I say. "My company transferred me there a few years back."

"Had yourself quite a night," Avery says. "Got any more little surprises for us?"

I apologize again and tell him no. I'll be on my way right after lunch, I say, if he'll be kind enough to lend me some clothes and get me to the bus station.

"Got any money?" he asks.

Amanda brings a pot of chili over to the table. She shouts for Brit who yells, "Coming!" from somewhere.

"I'll manage somehow," I say.

"He's out of work," Amanda says.

"Well, like I told you last night, I'll try my best to find you a secondhand engine. In fact, I'll swing by my junk man's yard later today, when I'm in Gonzales. But he only has one gear and that's slow." Avery spoons chili onto everyone's plate. "Meantime, you can make eight bucks an hour painting the station. That's what I'd pay Amanda's brother, if he'd ever get off his fat ass."

"I don't know, Avery," Amanda says. She turns to me. "Pardon me for saying so, but you don't exactly look like you're used to labouring in the sun."

Brit comes out of the bathroom then, wiping his hands on the seat of his pants. He slides onto Avery's lap and kisses him on the cheek.

"Well, are you up for it?" Avery asks me.

I think briefly about my job. My secretary has probably filled my voicemail box with Where-the-hell-are-you? messages. I had a big presentation to give today: The Secret to Success. The head office was flying salesmen in from all over the country to hear it. I peer around. There doesn't seem to be a phone in this kitchen. But these people must have a phone. My cell's still under the front seat. I have no idea whether it gets any bars here at the station.

I glance over at Amanda. She hasn't touched her plate. She's fiddling with a cracker, scraping off the salt crystals. I need to keep moving. Sharks that stop swimming drown.

"Amanda," I say, "If you want me to go, I won't impose on your hospitality any longer."

She looks at me long and hard. Then at Avery. Then at Brit. "Oh, I suppose it's alright—as long as you don't pull any more shit. And I mean that."

"I only had one razor," I say.

We all laugh; even Brit, who doesn't understand.

Avery and I are in the bedroom, surveying what's left of my suit. Amanda has already incinerated the jacket, shirt and tie. She's done a fair job of getting the blood out of the pants. They're certainly okay for painting. I start to put them on.

"Damn fool," Avery says, "you can't paint a gas station in those. They're made for sitting around with your legs crossed." He goes over to the closet and pulls out a pair of beat-up jeans. "There wasn't a better article of clothing ever made for a man than a pair of Levis."

"I don't think they'll fit," I say when he throws them at me.

"Sure they will." He crosses his arms and waits. I turn around and, with the bathrobe still wrapped around me, try pulling the jeans on. My left foot gets tangled in the robe and I stumble back into Avery, who laughs. "For Christ's sake, Alex, stop acting like an old lady. I've seen a man's dick before."

Reluctantly, I take the robe off. The jeans have holes in the knees and rips in the thighs. "I feel ridiculous," I say, turning to him, "These are too tight. I'll just wear my suit pants."

"Bullshit," Avery says, "That's the beauty of Levis. They put everything where it belongs." We're both looking down there. Better than looking into his eyes, I guess. Finally he turns to go. "I left a t-shirt under the bed yesterday," he says over his shoulder. "You're welcome to it, if you can stand my smell."

Before Avery leaves for Gonzales, he gives me a stepladder, a scraper, a couple of large brushes and two gallons of white latex. In front of me is the shady side of the service station, which Avery wants finished before supper. Behind me stretches Texas: nothing but a dirty dance floor disappearing into white hotness. My new universe is the triangle formed by this building, the two pumps in the middle of the yard, and a rust-and-neon Texaco sign at the side of the road. Beyond that, nothing but cacti and oil wells. Dallas. Other places I can never go back to. The Texaco sign buzzes and flashes: Last Chance for Gas or Water 30 Miles.

I lean the stepladder against the dead clapboards. May as well start on the eaves. The scraping part will go quickly; only a few mean flakes of ancient paint cling to this last chance Texaco. Amanda rounds the corner from the house. She's carrying a faded lawn chair, an empty colander, and a frying pan full of peas. I smile hello. She sets her chair in the shade, counseling me to stop and rest the minute I feel dizzy. I nod and begin. She sits and shells peas into the colander on her lap. Her cotton skirt is hiked up around her thighs. Its hem flutters, catching what little breeze there is. I think of the gauzy white · curtains in the bedroom. There's only one. One bedroom, a kitchen, a bath—the house is tiny. I wonder where I'll sleep tonight.

"So where did you say you were from?" Amanda asks.

"Dallas."

"I mean where in New York."

"Manhattan," I say, cautiously. "Midtown. Have you ever been?"

"Went to Julliard. Lived on Prince Street for a while." She dumps a pod of peas into the colander. Sounds like buckshot.

"The music school?"

"No, Julliard School of Agriculture," she says. "Christ, you are a New Yorker."

I apologize. I'm getting tired of apologizing for everything.

"Oh forget it," she says. "Even I find it hard to believe, it's been so long. I went there on scholarship for cello."

"Were you any good?" I ask.

She shrugs. "Won a few prizes. But I sucked at auditions."

"How did you end up out here?"

"Got pregnant," she says, popping a row of peas into her mouth. "Didn't want to give the baby up. Couldn't afford to stay in New York. So I decided to sell the Gagliano, come back home with my tail tucked between my legs, and buy this here filling station from my uncle."

"Did you meet Brit's father at Julliard?" I ask.

"You sure got a lot of questions for a guy with no past," she says. She has a point.

"Sorry." I climb down and move the ladder. Amanda motions me over. She tells me to open wide. She places a pea pod on my tongue. I crunch down on it. My lips close over her index finger by mistake.

"He was a handsome thing," she sighs. She pushes my face away and waves me back to the ladder. "Charles Benjamin Morrissey. Dressed really bohemian, but we all knew he had money. He took me to the MoMA once to see an exhibition on contemporary British portrait artists. There was this one painting, sort of done in a Hockney style, that looked exactly like Ben—that's what everybody called him—and sure enough, it was him. A friend of his from the Royal Academy had painted it." Amanda stops for a moment to suck on a pea pod. "Anyway," she says, "Ben and I auditioned for a lot of the same orchestra seats. He used to come over to my apartment to practice duets. Sure made my strings hum."

We both laugh.

"Where did you meet Avery?" I ask.

"Avery," she sighs, shading her eyes to look out into the heat from our precious slice of shade, "Avery and his red dog blew in on a dust storm one day. I needed someone to dig me a dry well. He's been here ever since. I kind of got used to his smile."

I do a double-take. Did she say smile or smell?

She searches the horizon, then continues. "Another long time ago, that was." But something in her tone has changed. I notice the peas are all shelled, but she's still searching the shimmering heat. "Sort of reminds you of a deserted island, doesn't it?" she says. I follow her gaze. There's nothing out there; not even a sound, except for the buzz and hum of the Texaco sign. She turns to me, then. "Avery's not much. But he helps out, helps pass the time." She gets up and folds the lawn chair, telling me supper's at six. She'll call me when it's ready.

The moon is so bright, I wake when a shadow tickles my face. Amanda stands naked and grateful in the cool stream of curtains created by a fan, staring out at blue Texas. I watch her from my makeshift bed of stacked blankets and sleeping bags on the floor. Only a thin top sheet separates us. She begins to braid her hair, slowly, which reminds me of a dream I sometimes have about living under the sea. In my dream there are mermaids and mermen living on a deserted island, all with the same slippery-smooth lower bodies of fishes. I almost say something, but hear Avery getting up from the bed. His shadow crosses too. He joins Amanda in the curtains, a waterfall of gauze. His hair is out of its ponytail and I marvel at how similar they look from behind. Cascades of hair over china blue skin. A blue Gemini. Avery takes over the braiding. Amanda begins to stroke her own breasts. Avery kisses her neck and twists, kisses her shoulder and twists, whispers into her ear and twists. Brit sleeps soundly at the foot of their bed. And I suffocate under this thin, white sheet.

**

I wake up this morning.

A little boy is wrapped in my arms. He is awake, but lying very still and staring at the wall.

"Where are we?" I whisper.

"In bed," he answers.

"In Texas?" I ask. The little boy nods. "I remember now," I say. He nods again, encouraging me.

"What are you doing here?" I whisper again.

"Sleeping," he says.

"But I thought you were sleeping in the big bed."

"I was."

I can't shake my dream. My legs have grown together and I'm sprouting fins and a tail.

"What time is it?" I ask Brit.

"Breakfast time," he says. All at once I get it, the quirky gravity of Middle of Nowhere, Texas. This underwater vertigo.

"Breakfast time," I repeat.

"Breakfast time," Brit giggles.

Before starting where I left off yesterday on the Texaco, I search the car for my cell phone. It isn't under the driver's seat. Neither is my wallet. Suddenly not having any money feels different than pretending not to have any. If I had a lick of sense I'd start walking, now; and I'd keep walking until I reached the Rio Grande. I check the glove compartment. The gun is gone.

Avery is sitting on a bench outside the office. "Looking for something?" he says. He's flipping though the photo sleeves of my wallet. "Who's this?" he asks. "She's pretty."

"That was my wife, Cathy."

"Was?"

"We're divorced," I say. My teeth are sticking to my lips.

"Still wearing the ring, though." Now he's counting the bills.

"It's all pretty recent," I say. "There's a little less than three hundred in there."

"Amanda doesn't get into Gonzales much," Avery says. "She generally avoids people like the plague. But Brit's busting out of his shoes, so she's fixing to do the weekly grocery run today instead of me, and then head over to Payless."

"So?"

"So if you're the front-page headline of all the newspapers, she'll probably find out about it."

I haven't seen a single newspaper lying around. No radio. No TV.

"You want me to leave?" I ask.

"I want you to finish the Texaco. But you may not have much choice in the matter by suppertime. Until then, if you want to be Alex, Alex you are. I don't give a rat's ass. Who's to say my name is Avery but me?"

I stand frozen to the spot. Melted, more like.

Avery stands. He tucks my wallet into the back pocket of his jeans. "Why don't you get started on the south side before the sun gets too hot? There won't be any shade. Switch to the front when you can't stand it anymore."

I can't move.

He smiles. "I'll put your wallet in the safe under the cash register," he says. "That's where I already put your gun. Brit likes to poke around in cars; he's going to make a hell of a mechanic one day—if he doesn't turn out to be a goddamn cellist."

I'm at the sink, finishing up the last of the lunch dishes. Amanda's making out her grocery list, checking cupboards. A determined odour—the scent of star anise—trails her around the kitchen. I alternate between watching her and staring out the window. Outside, Avery is playing with Blue, waiting for customers. Here in the kitchen, Brit is poring over a book at the kitchen table, waiting for Amanda.

"What are you reading?" I ask him, letting the soapy water drain out of the sink. My wrists have turned yellow and purple; but Amanda has dabbed the cuts with mercurochrome and Bag Balm. They seem to be healing.

"*Winnie-the-Pooh*," Brit says.

"What's going on over in Pooh Corners?"

"Tigger needs to be unbounced," he tells me.

"A matter of opinion," Amanda says. She is putting on a straw hat. She shoves her list into one of the pockets of her dress. "Ready to go, Brit?"

"You look pretty," Brit tells her, closing his book. She does.

"Poor thing," she laughs, "He doesn't have anyone to compare me to." But she pecks him on the cheek. She turns to me. "Behave yourself," she says. She hesitates before giving me a peck, too. "I expect to see the front of the station done when I get back."

"Yes ma'am," I say.

I can't remember: Do they ever manage to unbounce Tigger?

Avery is at the pumps, filling up a farmer's tractor. "Feel like switching jobs for the afternoon?" he asks. I shrug. It's his station—well, Amanda's. He shows me how to work the pumps. They're old and mechanical, nothing like the self-serve ones on the highway. An hour passes. I practice washing the windows of my own car with a squeegee. Still no customers. I watch Avery paint, his shirt off, lean torso covered in sweat. I'm thumbing through *Winnie-the-Pooh* when a dusty station wagon pulls into the yard. A fat lady gets out of the driver's seat. There's an old man in the passenger's side, but he doesn't move. He doesn't look like he's even breathing. "Where's Avery?" she asks, hands on her hips.

"Painting," I say. I point over at the station.

"Now that's a switch," she says, waving to Avery. "I heard it was Amanda's school friend from Back East who was painting this place. I'd like five dollars worth of regular. Check the oil while you're at it."

"We traded for the afternoon," I say. School friend? Who, me?

"None of my business, anyway," she says. "People are always saying more than their prayers. Staying long?"

"Depends, I guess."

"None of my business anyway," she says.

I pump the gas, check the oil. She hands me the exact amount out of a coin purse. She tells me to give her best to Amanda. The man in the passenger seat continues to stare down the road as they drive away.

More time passes. A Mercedes pulls up. Like mine, it's one of those expensive colours—titanium—not a colour but a sheen. I stare at myself in the mirrored windows: tanned, disheveled. I like this disguise. The last time I looked at myself was in the bathroom mirror, back in Dallas. I make a mental note to ask Avery why there are no mirrors at the Texaco. No radios, TVs, or telephones. No newspapers or mirrors.

The window hums down and I'm thrown a little off guard. It's as if I'm still staring back at my own, unblinking reflection. The driver is about thirty with dark hair and brown eyes. He's dressed in a business suit. He looks tired.

"What'll it be?" I ask.

"Fill it, please, with super-unleaded," he says.

"I'll give you as unleaded as I've got," I say. While his tank is filling, I begin washing the windshield. I can feel him staring at me from the other side of the glass. I smile in self-defense, but refuse to look inside, to see if he's smiling back. I concentrate on my own, smiling reflection. When the pump shuts off, I tell him how much it will be.

"Card or cash?" he asks. I say it's better to give me cash since this is my first day and I'm not sure how to work the credit card machine. He hands me a crisp twenty. No wedding ring.
"By the way," he says, putting my greasy change into his leather billfold, "Where the hell am I?" He smells of money and confidence. Cool controlled air emanates from the car's interior.

"If you lived here, you'd be home right now," I tell him, imagining I'm Avery. "My bet is you're a long way from home."

"You never know," he says, smiling.

"You never know," I agree.

His windows go back up, and he's back in climate control. He drives away. I only remember, too late, to check the license plate.

Not too long afterward, a dusty VW bus wheezes over to the pumps. A young woman climbs out of the driver's side.

"Hey!" she says.

"Hi there," I say. "Regular or unleaded?"

"This old deathtrap's got more gas in her than a Baptist potluck supper. But I smelled something funny as I was coming up the road. Thought I'd better check the fan belt."

"The fan belt," I say. There's no hood on the front of the bus. Old VW engines are in the back somewhere.

"New, huh?" she says. "Follow me."

She's dressed in an Indian print skirt, Houston Astros t-shirt and sandals. She has closely-cropped, copper-coloured hair and lots of freckles. She jangles slightly, but doesn't have any bracelets on. She's wearing what look like small, silver wind chimes in her ears. She pokes around in the grimy car guts without flinching. She doesn't seem to be getting dirty. I stand behind her, peering uselessly over her shoulder at the engine. A familiar sensation begins warming in my stomach.

"Where's the cute Tex-Mex who's usually on the pumps?" she asks. I tell her he's over there painting the station. She turns to me and whispers, "Half the women in the county drive out here just to be able to say, 'Fill-her-up!' " We both laugh. "Nope," she says. "It ain't the fan belt. Everything fine back here. Could use some water, though. Got a hose?"

"I'll have to bring some over in a jug," I tell her.

"Meantime, I'll just wash up and fetch me a Coke from the machine. Want one?"

"Okay," I say. "Key to the washroom's inside the door. Just grab the Cokes out of the fridge in the office. The machine's broken." I take an empty gallon jug over to the hose near where Avery's painting.

"Everything under control?" he asks from the ladder.

"Fine," I say.

"Her name's Callie. She lives all by herself in Gonzales," he says, climbing down. "Owns a little vegetarian sandwich shop. Does all right—not because there are so many vegetarians in town, just not a lot of sandwich shops." He sees me struggling with the knobs of the faucet. He takes the hose from my hand, jiggles the nozzle mysteriously, and water sprays out. "Needs to be cajoled," he says. Then he turns the hose on me.

I yelp and try to jump out of his aim. I bump into the sandwich shop lady, who's rounding the corner from the restroom. Avery turns the spray on her as well. She shrieks. Together, we try to grab the hose away from him. But Avery zigzags as far away as the hose will allow, turning it first on me then on her. Finally, I pin him against the wall. She wrestles the hose out of Avery's hand and drenches him—getting me in the process—and sticks the nozzle down the front of Avery's jeans. Avery surrenders. It takes us a while before we believe him.

The three of us sip Cokes on the front stoop while we dry off. Callie explains the VW's odd smell to Avery, and they figure out what the problem is. Avery promises to order a part and bring it by the sandwich shop next week. Callie will install it herself.

I sit as close to Callie as I can, inhaling her dampness. I feel as though I know this body; know where to tickle it, where to kiss it to make her sigh.

Suddenly an enormous image knifes its way to my consciousness. I struggle to stay in the sunlight and the laughter, but in a huge black eclipse I can see myself kicking open the door of my own bedroom. I am brandishing a new revolver, and its metallic sheen is pointed directly where Cathy lies naked. Her pale legs are tangled up in the sheets along with the slim brown ones of some dark-haired beauty. Cathy screams and scrambles out of bed. It's not what it looks like, she says. I watch as she stumbles over a giant pink dildo glistening on the carpet.

My Coke bottle shatters when it hits the cement. I rise to my feet and lurch inside the station with both Avery and Callie calling after me: Are you all right? But I can't answer—I'm choking—that giant pink dildo. Nothing is ever what it looks like.

When I saw it, I swear I started to howl: at my marriage, at what I'd become, at the fact that I'd never gotten around to taking the advanced seminar after the Secret to Success—The Big Picture. I just set that gun down on the dresser, loosened my tie and said, Make room for me girls.

I fling open the restroom door. I make it to the toilet just in time.

From the edge of the bed, I watch the room turn another, deeper shade of blue—an understanding, finally, of the colour indigo. The curtains rustle. Waves of blueness wash over me. My torso is bare, and the sweat from a stifling afternoon dries on my skin, tightens as it dries. Avery swapped jobs back after Callie left. I told him I was fine, that yesterday's chili didn't really agree with me. Then I painted and painted. I painted the station as if my very life depended on it.

A couple of days of scraping and painting have begun to tone up my biceps. I knead them and stifle a yawn. I'm so tired. I feel like undressing and crawling under the crisp white sheets. I picture myself drifting off to the undersea kingdom, with only my upper body exposed to the elements.

Avery walks in.

"Why are you sitting in the dark?" he asks, reaching for the switch.

"Don't. I like it," I say.

Avery shrugs and strolls over to the bedpost. His closeness seems to intensify the indigo molecules of the room, making them hum and hum and rebound off from one another.

"Sore?" he asks me.

I drop my hands to my lap, to Avery's borrowed jeans. "A little," I say. "I'm okay."

Avery jumps onto the bed and kneels behind me, his legs straddling either side of my hips. He begins to massage my shoulders.

"Why aren't there any mirrors?" I ask. My head rolls. I can't help it. I'm so tired.

No answer.

I can feel the heat of his body. From his breath on the back of my neck I learn the secret of his scent: sweat mixed with Amanda's star anise. His hands move to my biceps, then to my back. I become lost in the quiet hum of the fan, and in the even quieter hum which connects me to him. If he speaks I'll die and if he doesn't say something soon, I'll die. That hum. It rises in pitch to become a sort of wail, one that begins to resemble a police siren.

"Jesus Christ," Amanda says.

She's standing at the bedroom door. There's a Payless bag in her left hand, my revolver in her right. "That's enough, now," she says, aiming the gun at my head. "I won't let you make a fool out of me."

Acknowledgements

Nearly all of the stories in this collection were first published elsewhere. I'd like to acknowledge the following journals and anthologies for their support.

"Blood Pudding" originally appeared in *American Short Fiction* (Vol. 5, No. 18); "With Mirrors" in *Story* (Vol. 41, No. 4). Both pieces, as well as "Dan, In re: Christine" and "We're from HQ," were subsequently anthologized in Faber & Faber London's *First Fictions: Introduction 13*. "Lurid, Psychotic Colours" first appeared in the online literary journal *Crania* (Issue 4); and "Castaway" in LOSTmag.com (Summer 2006). "Blackjack" was originally published in *The New York Native* (Issue 297); "Black Tie" in *Southwest Review* (Vol. 91, No. 2); and "The Almond Eater" in *Metropolitan* (No. 8, Desire). "Loss of Gravity" was first published as "Framework of Loss" in *Neonlit: Time Out's Book of New Writing* (Vol. 1). Finally, the title for "Mise en Abîme" was inspired by a passage in Neal Kane's wonderful first novel *The Practice Life*. For the sake of continuity, I have occasionally taken the liberty of changing a character name or story setting from the way in which it was originally published.

This collection would not have been possible without the unflagging support of my friends at the Corporation of Yaddo, America's oldest and finest art colony. And it's a much better read thanks to the keen eye of Andrew Steinmetz; every author should have the chance to work with an editor who is also a terrific writer.

Finally, a heartfelt thank-you goes to the sculptor Timothy Horn for passing along two pieces of excellent advice for struggling artists: Seek your audience, and Pace yourself, it's a long career.

Art Corriveau

ESPLANADE
Books

THE FICTION SERIES AT VÉHICULE PRESS

[Esplanade Editor: Andrew Steinmetz]

A House by the Sea
A novel by Sikeena Karmali

A Short Journey by Car
Stories by Liam Durcan

Seventeen Tomatoes: Tales from Kashmir
Stories by Jaspreet Singh

Garbage Head
A novel by Christopher Willard

The Rent Collector
A novel by B. Glen Rotchin

Dead Man's Float
A novel by Nicholas Maes

Optique
Stories by Clayton Bailey

Out of Cleveland
Stories by Lolette Kuby

Pardon Our Monsters
Stories by Andrew Hood

Blood Pudding
Stories by Art Corriveau

Véhicule Press
www.vehiculepress.com